Stealing
Jason Wilde

ALSO BY DEE ERNST

Stealing Jason Wilde

DEE ERNST

LAKE UNION
PUBLISHING

Text copyright © 2016 Dee Ernst
All rights reserved.

Published by Lake Union Publishing, Seattle

www.apub.com

Amazon, the Amazon logo, and Lake Union Publishing are trademarks of Amazon.com, Inc., or its affiliates.

ISBN-13: 9781503935501
ISBN-10: 1503935507

Printed in the United States of America

This book is for the Tabor Ladies:
Cory, Sue, Jean, Michele, Cheri, Mel, Karen,
Diane, Ellen, and my cousin, Lisa, who managed
to sneak in there at the last minute. Thank you
for the years of laughter and friendship, as well as
many memorable girls' weekends.

I always felt sorry for anyone who wasn't in our
company. We were—and still are—always sitting at
the Cool Kids Table.

Chapter One

You know that famous saying "What happens on Dune Road stays on Dune Road"?

Wait—maybe it's really not that famous. The famous version is about Las Vegas. But are you familiar with the concept? That there are some places in the world where your choices are based on a completely different reality and your actions have no consequences in your day-to-day life? Where you are allowed, even encouraged, to behave in a different way, and, above all, it is understood that that those two separate worlds must *never* intersect?

That's 461 Dune Road. It began as a joke, of course. Seriously, how much trouble could a bunch of fiftyish ladies from Hopewell, New Jersey, get into in the Hamptons? Especially before Memorial Day, when the place is practically deserted (because we *never* could have afforded to spend a whole week in a beach house in Westhampton Beach during the high season).

But we always said it, on those first nights together, after we'd unpacked all our stuff and opened the wine and trooped out to the beach with those cute red plastic cups. We'd stand right at the edge of the ocean, ankles turning blue from the cold water, and toast to another ladies' week away, and one of us would always say, "Remember, what happens on Dune Road stays on Dune Road."

Then we would all laugh.

Because in six years, nothing had ever happened that warranted such a dire oath.

But then, of course, something did.

We hadn't started out spending an entire week in a Hamptons beach house. When my daughter was six, she invited her two best friends for a sleepover. I invited the moms, Deb Esposito and Kelly Castellano. The girls watched Disney movies and ate cookies. We watched old musicals, drank too much wine, and laughed ourselves silly. We continued the tradition, even as my daughter invited more and more friends. I just kept inviting more and more moms. One year, my lovely daughter asked that I *not* invite the moms to her next party because we, the moms, were too loud and rowdy.

That was when we started checking into local hotels and, as our kids got older, moved from one night away to a whole weekend, in places like New Hope and Woodstock and as far away as Boston. By the time we found the house on Dune Road, we had clinched a whole week away. At one point, there were eight of us going off every year, leaving our husbands and teenagers behind.

But—kids grow up and move out of the house. Husbands and wives decide to part company. Stuff happens. Although the week at Dune Road had become something of a standing holiday, there finally came a year where Kelly, Deb, and I were the only ones going, and we were all just a little bit bummed.

I was still Annie Reynolds. No, I never took my maiden name back after the divorce. For one thing, I was too lazy. Who wanted to fill out all those name-change forms? And I had liked being Mrs. Reynolds. My marriage had not been some terrible thing. It had just been a thing with a limited shelf life, like dry goods or produce. Except with children.

We had the usual organizational meeting at a local pub, where the music was geared to baby boomers and I never felt like the oldest person in the room. We ordered nachos, drank wine, and pretended to make notes.

"I can't believe everyone just blew us off like that," Deb groused.

Kelly had a mouthful of nachos, so she swallowed carefully before speaking. "Well, Jen's son getting married is not exactly a feeble excuse."

"There are fifty-two weeks in the year," Deb pointed out. "He had to pick *this* one? And Marie and her anniversary thing—she's missed every other anniversary to spend the week with us. Why back out this year?"

"Well," I said, "it is her twenty-fifth. That's kind of a big deal. And Gary surprised her with a cruise."

"Again," Deb said, "fifty-two weeks?" She waved her hand, silver rings flashing. "He never did like her going away with us. He did that on purpose, you know. To keep her from coming with us."

"Or maybe," I said, "he did it because it's the week of their actual anniversary?"

Deb made a noise that expressed both disbelief and contempt.

"You're not going to back out on us too, are you?" Kelly asked me.

"Hey, I have always gone to Dune Road," I reminded her. "Even the year that Joe left."

"Yes," Deb said slowly. "But you've gotten a lot more, ah, withdrawn lately."

I stared at her in surprise. "What are you talking about?"

Kelly shrugged. "Let's face it, Annie. You're kind of in your own little world these days."

I tried to look like I didn't know what she was talking about, but I did. I preferred to think of my situation as "a perfected routine." A very narrow and predictable routine, perhaps, but one that was working for me and I saw no reason to disrupt. I had gotten used to my lists and schedules. I was comfortable with Chinese food every Thursday, and grocery shopping on Sunday mornings. Some would call my life boring. Maybe. But it was also safe.

"Dune Road is right up there with Christmas and the Saint Patrick's Day parade," I told them. "Written in stone. You know that."

Kelly sighed happily. "Okay, then. The good news is that, with just the three of us, we'll each get our own room this year." Kelly, at just fifty, was the baby of the group and had been divorced barely a year. She had just begun to talk about dating again.

"The big thing, of course, is the money," Deb said sadly. She was an RN, had been working at the same hospital for more than twenty years, and was easily making six figures a year. But with her youngest in graduate school and her older daughter graduating and starting to make getting-married noises, she was watching every penny.

I nodded. "Of course. It always is." I drank more wine. I was living on a librarian's salary, and my alimony would be running out in a year. Money should have been my concern as well, but as part of my life plan to remain wrapped in a warm blanket and stay snug and complacent in my burrow, I was in total denial. "I was thinking that maybe we could ask Tina."

Tina Malcolm had moved out of Hopewell five years ago, after she'd divorced her husband and relocated to Hoboken, where, she said, she could more easily pursue her career. We'd all been a bit surprised, because she had never worked as long as we'd known her, except for her slavish devotion to Mary Kay. She had been with us on a few of our earlier expeditions, and went with us on our first trip to Dune Road, six years ago. That had been the last time she'd gone with us.

"Tina is a whack job," Kelly muttered.

"No, she's not," I said, although I had to admit that Tina kind of was. "She was a lot of fun in Woodstock."

"Where she tried to pick up our busboy," Deb pointed out, "who was only seventeen. We all could have gone to jail for that one."

"She was drunk," I said.

"So was I," Deb said. "But I managed to control myself."

"Her OCD will drive me nuts," Kelly said.

"She's on new meds," I said.

"For her anxiety too?" Kelly asked. "You know how she gets in crowds."

"Oh, and then there's her bridge aversion, remember?" Deb said. "How can she drive to the Hamptons? We have to go over a bridge. Unless we fly."

Kelly shook her head. "She can't fly either."

"I talked to her just last week," I explained. "She said she was doing great and really wanted to join us this year. She hasn't seen us since— when?—Deb's fiftieth? And that was three years ago."

"She is fun," Deb said slowly. "But why this year? She hasn't asked to come with us in years, not since that first year on Dune Road."

I sighed. "It's because of Jason Wilde. They film his cable series in Sag Harbor, and she thinks there's a chance we'll run into him."

Kelly snorted. "Is she kidding? How long have we been trying to bump into Ina Garten? Celebs don't walk around the streets of Sag Harbor. That will never happen."

"Who's Jason Wilde?" Deb asked.

"An actor. Not a very good one, if I remember correctly. He was really big in the late nineties, I think," I said. "Had that detective show with the cute dog? I think the dog was a better actor than he was. But he was charming, you know? And then he made a bunch of really bad movies."

"He was naked in most of them," Kelly said with a faraway look on her face. "Full frontal."

"That's right," I said. "God, he was good-looking."

Deb glanced at me. "You're not dating anyone right now, are you?"

I shrugged. "Are you kidding?" I shook my head. "I haven't dated anyone since 1982."

"Yeah, what about that? You've been divorced for a while now," Deb said. "Why aren't you out there fishing around?"

Joe had left me three years earlier, and now that both of my kids were off on their own, I had found myself quite comfortable living alone. I had dabbled with online dating sites. Men my age wanted twentysomethings. I did get a lot of attention from a spry seventy-six-year-old, but I could never commit to a face-to-face meeting, especially after he admitted that his online photo was twelve years old. The few dates I did go on went nowhere. And since I rarely went out of the house for a social occasion that did not involve my kids or a girls'-night dinner, I had failed thus far to "meet cute" any remotely promising gentleman of acceptable age.

"I have no interest in dating again at my age. The last time I had a man in my life, it did not end well. And how would I even start? I'm too old to hang out in bars, and all my friends' older brothers are married to twenty-year-olds. Besides, I'm way past the desired demographic."

I stared at my wine. Should I finish in one gulp, or pour the remaining half glass over my head in a pathetic display of middle-age angst?

"Ann, that's not true," Kelly said. "Maybe you and Tina and I can go trolling for men one night. I bet there are some great guys in the Hamptons."

"That would involve going out and hanging around in bars," I grumbled. "I'm too old for that. I just told you, remember?"

"We used to do it all the time," Deb reminded me. "We'd always find a little place out there where we'd have a few drinks and sing with the band and get up and dance."

"Yes, but we were married then," I said. "It was all in fun. We could flirt and dance and know it wasn't going anywhere. But now? Now we're on a mission. To find a man. And since I do not need a husband or boyfriend to feel happy and complete, I'd feel like I was just trolling for sex."

"And what the hell is wrong with that?" Kelly asked.

I chose to ignore her. "Besides, you and Tina are both so much prettier than I am. And younger. And skinnier," I pointed out. "Whoever we meet will automatically start fighting over the two of you. You know me—it will take me three drinks to get up enough nerve to even start a conversation, and by then everyone will have gone home."

"First of all, you are still a looker, and no one would guess you're older than Tina, who *is* skinnier than you, but only because she's naturally built like a twelve-year-old boy," Deb said to me. "Kelly will get first choice, that's a given, but the good-looking one will probably have a really nice wingman, and I'll bet you'd be a real contender there."

"And then what would I do with him? I told you, I don't need another husband," I said.

Deb made a rude noise. "Do whatever you want, Ann. You're a grown woman. Sleep with him. Have a fling. You don't need another husband? Fine, I get that. But I bet you could use a little fun and excitement." She was right there. I hated when that happened. "And Kelly here needs to get her feet wet in the dating pool," Deb added.

We mulled this idea over for a few minutes, drinking, of course, more wine.

"So, I guess we'll invite Tina?" Kelly said.

We all nodded.

"Are we sure?" Deb asked. "I never understood why you even remained friends with her, Annie. Tina has always been a little off-center."

"I know," I said. "But she has a good heart. I mean, she went out of her way to spend time with me after Joe left, and she's always kept in touch."

We ordered another round.

"Well, you'd better make sure Tina understands that we have to pack light," Kelly said. "She's liable to bring three trunks full of designer duds."

"I'll explain the situation to her," I told them. "I'm sure she'll be fine."

Deb reached over and patted my hand. "That's what I love about you the most, Annie. Your total belief in your fellow man." She smiled broadly.

I threw her a look. "Is that sarcasm?"

She nodded. "Of course. It's how I roll."

We had, over the years, gotten the routine down to a science. We knew what to pack and what to expect at the house. Since it was just as easy to buy paper towels on Long Island as it was in New Jersey, we didn't pack household items anymore, but waited to see what was left over at the house, made a list, and bought whatever was needed at the Stop & Shop. One thing that was much cheaper to buy in Jersey was liquor, and it was the only thing besides clothes that we brought from home.

Kelly was actually making notes. "I've got two twelve-packs," she said. "Blue Moon okay? We'll have to remember oranges." She flipped through her notepad. "I'll add it to my list."

"Okay. Deb and I are splitting the wine," I said. "And, of course, we can always go to Milland Vineyard for that lovely ice wine."

Kelly, still scribbling furiously, began to blush.

Deb raised an eyebrow. "And I imagine you'd like to say hello to that lovely ice-wine maker?"

Kelly shook her head, but Deb poked her with the tip of her shoe. "You've been flirting with him for years. Now that you're finally divorced, you can crank up the charm, drop a few subtle hints, and I bet by the end of the week, he'll ask you to move out there."

Kelly flashed a naughty grin. "You know, there's something to that. After all, he's been very nice to fantasize about. It's that great butt of his. Maybe I will take him up on one of his many offers of sexual delight." Deb snorted.

Kelly and her flirtation with Liam the Wine Guy was an ongoing joke. Watching the two of them spar was like watching an old Meg Ryan romantic comedy.

"Montauk this year, okay?" Kelly said. "We haven't been back there since our first Hamptons trip."

Deb rolled her eyes. "That's because there's nothing there except the lighthouse, and we have bigger and better ones here at the Jersey shore."

"No, I liked Montauk," I said. "And there was that funky hotel, right? The ones the Rolling Stones sang about?"

"Memory Motel," Kelly said. "With that really great bar where Deb adopted that kid."

"I did not adopt him," Deb shot back. "He was lonely because his wife and babies were out of town for the weekend."

I laughed. "There you go. Trust Deb to have some guy try to pick her up, and she ends up going all Dr. Phil on him."

Deb shook her head. "He was not trying to pick me up. He thought I was the motherly type, and he needed a shoulder to cry on. We talked about being lonely and how he'll feel when his kids finally move out of the house."

People did not usually cry on Deb's shoulder. She was short and pleasantly plump, with skin the color of coffee with just a drop or two of cream, and gray hair in a neat Afro. She favored lots of silver and bead jewelry, and her nails were always painted bright coral. She looked like an African American Earth Mother, which was misleading. She was fiercely devoted to her family and friends, but she was not always kind or understanding toward strangers. She had an uncanny ability to see the worst possible scenario in any situation. Working in the ER could do that to a person. That, coupled with her flair for sarcasm, sometimes made her hard to take. But I loved her anyway.

"Okay," I said. "Are we done here? Anything else we should talk about?"

Everyone shook their heads.

"Good," Deb said, rubbing her hands together. "Did you hear about Donna and Tommy Jay?"

Kelly leaned in. "What?"

And we were off.

The next morning I stopped at the beauty salon. My hair was fairly long, past my shoulders, and dark brown. I had not paid much attention to my appearance lately. I usually bundled my hair on top of my head and got out of the house without too much time spent looking in the mirror. But when I went to the Hamptons, I made sure it was freshly cut and styled. There was something about spending a week surrounded by the wealthy and beautiful that made me want to step up my game.

"Hi, Bella," I called as I entered the salon. Bella had been cutting my hair for almost ten years by then. I followed her whenever she moved from salon to salon, not because she was such a good stylist, but because Bella was used to my thick, curly hair and I never had to explain how to cut it.

"And where have you been?" Bella asked. "I haven't seen you since before Christmas."

"Busy," I said, which was technically not a lie, as I had spent the last few months binge-watching *Lost* on Netflix. "It's Hamptons time again. What would you suggest?"

She took out my sloppy bun and pulled my hair down. She flattened the hair around my part, and I could see a broad stripe of gray. She fingered the ends of my hair, shaking her head.

"I suggest you pull your head out of the sand and pay attention to your life, Ann. You look old and tired with this head."

"Well, I feel old and tired, so it makes sense."

She shook her head. "Seriously, what are you doing to yourself? With the right cut and highlights, you could look ten years younger."

"And what can you do to make me *feel* ten years younger?"

"A facial. And a bikini wax."

"What? Why would a bikini wax make me feel younger?"

She smiled wickedly at my reflection. "Because you'll always be thinking that, if a handsome stranger asks, you can have sex with the lights on."

"I didn't do that when I was *twenty* years younger."

She sighed. "At least a facial. And a cut and color. Highlights? Please, let me do something here."

I nodded. It was easier than arguing.

Three hours later, I finally left. I did feel better. I also looked better. So much better, in fact, that I was almost inspired to buy a new outfit or two, but I could take only so much excitement in a day. I stopped for Chinese takeout on the way home. I thought about swinging by Kelly's to ask if she wanted to share my General Tso's, but decided to just eat at home alone.

Again.

It had taken me a while to get used to being a single person. I hadn't been one since I was sixteen. That was when I met Joe. We dated through high school, college, lived together for a year, then married. We had always had lots of ups and downs, but three years ago, he finally sat me down and told me that although he would always love me, he wasn't *in* love with me anymore. Instead of being shaken to the core, I was relieved. Our divorce was more amicable than the last years of our marriage had been.

I was not exactly happy with my life, but I was comfortable. I felt safe. Most of the time, it didn't bother me to think that the best part of my life was over. And then I'd think about it again and it *would* bother me. A lot.

I was a great planner, by the way. My laptop was filled with trips I'd carefully mapped out and descriptions of seminars I knew I'd love, and my planner was crammed with saved pages of classes, museum specials, and walking tours. But for some reason, I had a hard time getting past the planning stage. It was just easier to look at everything from the comfort of my own couch than to actually go out and do anything. But I was beginning to think I was approaching a now-or-never time in my life. If I didn't get out there and do something soon, I'd end up a ninety-year-old singleton, my butt permanently affixed to my couch, laptop melded with my thighs.

But how in the world does a fiftysomething, divorced empty nester find adventure, excitement, and—dare I say it—romance?

Certainly not in Hopewell, New Jersey.

Maybe, just maybe, on Dune Road.

Chapter Two

Tina had told me she'd drive over from Hoboken. In the past, Tina had been a little careless with time, but that Sunday morning she pulled into the driveway at ten o'clock sharp. I was loading my suitcase and a case of wine into the back of the van. Tina got out of her car, waving excitedly. She looked tiny—very thin, wearing one of those skintight dresses that appeared to be made of spandex—and tottered over on stilettos.

"You look so good," she squealed, hugging me tightly.

"You look good too, but completely different. Love the hair." Not really. It was cut very short and dyed that reddish-maroon that rock stars seemed to like. She was ten years younger than I was but looked like a twentysomething. I examined her closely. "Did you have something done? And why are your eyes green?"

She fluttered a hand. "A lifestyle lift. And Botox, of course. And since I have to wear contacts anyway, I might as well get some real good out of them."

"A lift? You're not even fifty."

"I know, but why wait? By fifty, it's too late."

I sighed. Thanks, Tina.

She scuttled around to the back of her Fiesta, opened the trunk, and pulled out a fairly large suitcase on wheels. I hurried over to help her, but as I rounded the back of the car, I stopped dead.

"What's all that?" I asked, staring into the trunk.

There was another suitcase, two pillows, two tote bags, a box from a liquor store filled with bottles of what looked like tequila, and a twelve-pack of toilet tissue.

"My stuff."

"Tina, we're there for only a week. And there's a washer and dryer. And pillows."

"I can't sleep on just any pillows. And I need all my clothes. I have to be prepared."

"For what?"

"Anything. You never know what might happen."

"What's in the tote bags?"

"Shoes."

"How many?"

"Nine pairs."

"Tina, we have limited space, I told you that. We have to get every-body's luggage into one van. There's no room for nine pairs of shoes. And what's with the toilet paper?"

"I can only use paper that's made with no dyes or additives."

"Additives? Are you kidding? What can you add to toilet paper?"

"Oh, you'd be surprised. My skin is very sensitive."

Of course it was. "Tina, if we put all this in the van, there won't be room for anybody else's stuff."

"We can pile it on top of the car. Don't you have bungee cords?"

"Yeah. Okay, I mean, I guess. How much tequila did you bring?"

"Eight bottles."

"Who's going to be drinking that much?"

"Well, we might have company."

I stared at her. "Like who? Or are you expecting Jason Wilde to stop by for a shot with lemon?"

Tina stopped struggling with the toilet paper long enough to give me a playful push. "Oh, Annie, stop. There's nothing wrong with being prepared for all contingencies."

I glanced at my watch. "We have to pick up Kelly and Deb in five minutes. Let's go."

The two of us wrestled Tina's stuff into the back of the van. Kelly, I knew, managed with one carry-on bag and a tote. We could put the twelve-packs in the middle of the backseat. Deb usually had one regular-size suitcase stuffed to the gills. With some strategic packing, we'd be fine.

"Okay, that's it. Get in while I lock up the house," I said. I ran in, made sure everything was locked up, grabbed my purse, and then hurried out. I hopped into the car—and jumped right back out again when I saw something moving on the floorboard.

"What is that?" I yelled.

"Muffy," Tina said above the din.

Muffy was a tiny Yorkshire terrier with a pink bow on top of her head. She was yapping loudly.

I closed my eyes and took a deep breath. "Tina, why did you bring a dog?"

"What else was I going to do with her?"

"I don't know. But you could have warned me. I mean, how do you know dogs are even allowed at the house? What if we get told to leave midweek? Tina, this is not a good idea."

She shrugged as she snuggled the now-growling Muffy against her flat chest. "I looked up the house online, and the owner made a point of saying it was dog-friendly."

"But you didn't ask any of us. What if we didn't want a dog?" I slid back into the car and pulled out of the drive. Muffy's noisemaking was down to a low snarl.

Tina fluttered her hand again. "Who wouldn't want a sweetie like this? And she loves the beach." She reached down into the huge, open purse at her feet and drew out a plastic bag filled with what looked like tiny bones. She gave one to Muffy, who crunched a few times, leaving crumbs on the car seat, which Tina brushed to the floor.

I turned the corner and started down the hill. "I didn't even know you had a dog."

"Oh," she cooed, "Muffy is so much more than a dog."

I glanced at Muffy, who bared tiny teeth. "Is she also a barracuda?"

"Silly."

I pulled into Kelly's driveway. Her stuff was on the porch. I beeped the horn, and she and Deb came hurrying out.

I got out and popped open the back of the van. Deb got to the van first and stared.

"Are you kidding?" she said.

Tina had gotten out, and now she threw her arms around Deb's neck. "I'm so happy to see you!" she squealed.

Deb dropped her suitcase and returned the hug. "Tina, baby, it's good to see you too, but what did you bring? You know we stay only a week, right?"

Tina repeated her hello-how-are-you dance with Kelly, who gave me a look over the top of Tina's head.

"Deb," I said, "I was thinking we could put the beer on the seat between you two in back, and maybe Kelly's tote on the floor."

Deb had moved a few things around in the back of the van and managed to get her suitcase in. "Well, we can try. If not, I'll just bungee-cord myself across the hood, like a dead deer," she said, and went off to get the beer.

Kelly's bag took up the last available inch of space, and when I closed the back of the van, I might have heard a crunch.

Kelly opened the car door, struggling with her tote bag, and screamed, "Annie, there's a rat in your van!"

"No, that's not a rat," I told her, taking the tote and pushing the snarling Muffy out of the way. "It's Muffy."

Kelly turned to Tina. "Why did you bring a dog?"

Tina shouldered her way past us and grabbed Muffy. "Because she's going to be so much fun."

Deb was coming toward us, staggering under the weight of too much beer. I grabbed the top twelve-pack, and we got everything packed in nicely. I got behind the wheel.

"Okay, so we're set?" she asked.

Tina pushed Muffy at me. "No. I really need to pee."

Kelly sighed, unlatched her seatbelt, got out of the van, and led Tina into the house.

Deb and I sat in silence. Except for Muffy, who was still snarling.

"This is a first," Deb said at last.

"What? The dog?"

She shook her head. "No. I already need a drink, and we haven't even left town."

We were doing fine until we got to the bridge.

I hated driving. Seriously. But I'd made a pact with myself after my divorce to get out of my comfort zone, and driving long distances was part of the plan.

Usually, there wasn't much traffic on the Throgs Neck Bridge on a Sunday morning. There never had been in previous years. So when things started slowing down, I wasn't too worried.

Besides, Tina was on new meds, right? She once told us she hadn't been to New York City in eight years because she was afraid to cross the George Washington Bridge. When someone suggested using one of the tunnels instead, she'd started hyperventilating.

We had decided on a radio station. We'd laughed at the vast expanse of dark storm clouds in front of us because Kelly's phone insisted that there was no rain in the forecast. Tina had told us stories of her crazy neighbors in her condo building and had us laughing out loud. Muffy had stopped snarling.

And then the van went from six miles an hour to a complete stop.

It took Tina a few minutes to notice, because she was turned around in her seat, talking to Deb and Kelly about a samples-only shop she'd found where you could buy $1,200 shoes for half price.

Deb had never even *looked* at a pair of $1,200 shoes in her entire life, but she was making polite noises anyway.

Then Tina turned to say something to me and noticed the long line of stopped traffic stretching before us.

"Why are we stopped?" she asked.

I relaxed my death grip on the steering wheel, then threw the van into park. "No idea. Probably work being done somewhere. There's usually not a lot of volume on the weekends."

Tina's Botoxed lips formed a thin line. Well, as thin as two bee-stung lips could get. "I don't like bridges."

"Let me check," Kelly said. I glanced over my shoulder. Kelly was on her phone again. She lived and breathed by the information she gleaned from her phone.

Tina shifted in her seat, her panic escalating. "Where are we?"

"On the Throgs Neck," I told her.

"Yes, but *where* on the Throgs Neck? I mean, are we almost at the end? Halfway?"

"Does it matter?" Deb asked from the backseat. "We're stuck. Anyone want a beer?"

Tina shivered delicately. "It's not even eleven o'clock."

"True," Deb said. "And if we're here awhile, peeing could be a problem."

"We're going to be here awhile," Kelly announced. "It's a stalled car. Just happened."

As if on cue, we heard sirens.

"How on earth do they expect to get through all this?" Tina asked.

I sat back a little farther into my seat. "No clue."

"Can we turn around?" Tina asked.

I stared at her. "Look where we are, Tina. Notice that concrete divider there? Kinda hard to drive over something like that."

That was the wrong thing to say. She craned her neck to look past me and the two lanes of traffic next to her. When she realized I wasn't lying and there *was* a concrete divider, her shoulders slumped. Then she looked to the other side, gasped, and whipped her head back facing front.

"There's water," she gasped, beginning to hyperventilate.

"Tina," Kelly said calmly, "of course there's water. It's a *bridge*."

Tina bent down, then started rummaging through her huge bag, squishing Muffy in the process, who began to whimper, then yelp. Tina straightened up, a silver flask in her hand.

"What's that?" I asked as she unscrewed the top.

"Vodka," she answered shortly, taking a quick sip.

"It's not even eleven o'clock," Deb piped up from the back.

Muffy was licking the side of the flask where vodka was dripping down.

"I don't like bridges," Tina said again. She thrust the flask at me, and I took it from her as she dived back into her bag. Muffy started yelping again. Tina grabbed the dog around her belly and practically threw her into the backseat. Kelly caught the dog as she fell, and Muffy promptly segued from yelping to outright barking.

"What are you looking for?" I asked.

Tina straightened. She had a pill bottle in her hand.

"I'm fine," she announced. She tipped the bottle, extracted two pills, snapped the top back on, and dropped the bottle back into her purse. Then she grabbed the flask from me, popped the pills, and washed them down with a long drink.

She closed her eyes and held the flask to her chest.

"I thought you said she was on meds," Kelly yelled from the backseat. Muffy began to whimper.

Traffic moved. I started the van, and we inched forward about two car lengths, then came to another full stop.

I looked over at Tina. Her eyes were tightly closed, and she was clutching the flask so hard that her knuckles were white. "Tina?"

She opened her eyes slowly, then stared straight ahead. "I thought we were moving," she said.

"I thought you were okay with going over the bridge," Deb said.

Tina nodded, and said through a wildly fake smile, "I'm fine. Really. The bridge is not going to collapse. The bridge is *not* going to collapse." She kept up this mantra, saying it over and over while slightly swaying back and forth.

Oh, my God. I'd never thought about that. I mean, when was the last time a bridge collapsed that wasn't a result of a natural disaster, like an earthquake? And when was the last time there was an earthquake on Long Island? "Of course it's not," I told her, in my very best Mary Poppins voice. "And look, we're moving again."

It took us about six minutes to go twenty feet. Not bad, really.

And then it started to rain. A lot.

Thunder boomed and lightning flashed, and the rain came down so hard we couldn't see out the windows. I put the wipers on turbo, but we still couldn't see a thing.

Tina started to hum to herself.

"Why don't you take Muffy," Kelly suggested. "It's a scientific fact that petting a dog is a very calming activity."

I watched as Muffy tumbled down Tina's shoulder onto her lap. Tina grabbed the dog so hard Muffy growled.

"Good dog," Tina said, her eyes shut tight again. She was stroking the dog, but with the same hand she was using to hold her flask, so poor Muffy kept getting hit on the back with it.

We sat for a few minutes. The radio could not drown out the sound of the pounding rain, the crackle of lightning, or the thunder. Or the steady beat of the windshield wipers. Then, traffic moved another four feet.

"If lightning strikes the bridge, what will happen?" Tina asked between clenched teeth.

"Oh, my God," Deb mumbled. "If I'm lucky, we'll be instantly incinerated." We heard the familiar pop of a beer can being opened.

"I'll look it up," Kelly said brightly. I could hear her fingernails clicking against her phone. "Not to worry. There's enough rubber in the average car to absorb any shock," Kelly said at last. "We're very safe."

Tina nodded several times. She must have realized she was petting the dog with her flask, because she suddenly stopped and opened her eyes.

She smiled. "Better now."

"Thank you, Jesus," Deb said quietly.

Tina visibly relaxed in her seat. Whatever she'd taken had kicked in. She smiled, leaned forward to drop her flask in her purse, and pulled out her phone.

Was she calling her therapist?

She made kissing noises at Muffy.

"Men are four times more likely than women to get hit by lightning," Kelly said, still reading her phone. "A lot of them get hit while fishing."

"Imagine that," Deb said. I glanced in the rearview mirror. Deb was downing her beer.

"Yes," Kelly continued. "About two thousand people get struck each year."

I shifted my eyes to Kelly. She was scrolling down the screen of her phone. We moved ahead another twenty feet.

Now, Tina was making a call.

"Hello? Is this the state police?" she asked.

I hit the brakes and stared at her.

"My name is Tina Malcolm," she said sweetly. "And I have a huge favor to ask. I'm on the Throgs Neck Bridge—"

"What?" Deb yelped. She leaned forward to grab Tina's arm. Tina swatted her hand away.

"Yes, sir, I am in a car, but there's a stalled vehicle, and traffic has completely stopped, and I have a few . . . anxiety issues," Tina went on. "Would it be possible for you to send someone to get me across the bridge right away?"

Deb slumped back. I saw her reach for another beer. Kelly actually put down her phone and leaned forward.

"Tina, are you crazy?" Kelly hissed.

What a question.

"No, Officer, you don't understand," Tina said, her voice a little sharper. *"We're stuck on the bridge."*

I could hear the rumble of a voice on the other end of the phone. Tina's jaw clenched.

"Well, what about a helicopter, then?" she asked.

Amazing. Whoever was on the other end was actually trying to reason with her, raising the idea of "public servant" to a whole new level.

"I see," she said, her hand tightening around her smartphone. "Well, that's not very helpful, is it? After all, I do contribute to your paycheck. You could try being a bit more sympathetic."

She rolled her eyes, then let the phone fall onto her lap, hitting Muffy in the eye, causing the dog to start yelping again.

"Hey, Tina," Deb said, "could I take a hit from your flask?"

Tina wordlessly pulled the flask from her bag, handing it back to Deb. Her foot was tapping, and her fingers were patting Muffy on the head.

"Are you still fine?" I asked her.

Tina nodded. I looked in the rearview mirror at Deb. Deb caught my eye, shook her head, then took a swig of vodka.

We moved forward another few feet.

"So, Tina," Kelly said, "I haven't seen Jason Wilde's TV show myself. How is it?"

Tina's face softened, and she smiled dreamily. "He plays a disgraced, wrongfully dismissed LA homicide detective who moves to Sag Harbor and becomes a yoga instructor, but he helps his clients with problems on the side. You know, blackmail and kidnapping. He even solves murders."

"Imagine," Deb muttered. "I've seen nothing but white people in the Hamptons. Are you sure about murders?"

"Oh, yes," Tina said. "And there are lots of African Americans in the Hamptons. At least on his show. They aren't just criminals, of course."

I glanced in the rearview mirror in time to see Deb roll her eyes.

Tina continued as she cuddled Muffy, scratching the dog's belly, causing frantic tail wagging. "I don't imagine the show is very realistic. I mean, I doubt a yoga instructor could afford a beachfront house with a pool. He spends lot of time there, running in and out of the surf. And climbing in and out of his pool. Wet, you know." Her voice got dreamy. "Of course, he spends a lot of his time in his yoga studio, shirtless and in very unusual positions."

"That sounds so interesting. I'll have to check it out," Kelly said.

"Oh, it's a great show. And because it's cable, he's naked too. Just his ass, sadly, but he's lovely. And, you know, wet."

"God bless cable," Deb said. I heard the pop of another beer can opening.

Traffic started moving again. I squinted through the rain, concentrating on not running into the car in front of me. It took us about ten minutes to get to the stalled car, which was in the center lane, so all the traffic was funneled into the left lane. Once we passed the car, we picked up speed.

The rain eased up a bit and the lightning stopped.

"Okay, ladies," I sang out. "We're on our way."

I glanced at Tina, who was now slumped forward in her seat, asleep.

"The forecast has changed," Kelly said. "Looks like rain for the next three days."

"Perfect," I muttered. "Anything else?"

"Yeah," Deb said. "I really have to pee."

Chapter Three

There are some amazing restaurants in the Hamptons, world-class and well known, where the rich and famous hang out on a regular basis. You've probably read about them, seen the reviews, and gazed in wonder at glossy photos in expensive travel magazines of fabulous-looking food. You may have wished that you could sit down at a corner table covered in crisp white linen and taste that amazing food, while glancing over to the next table and nodding casually to Spielberg or Seinfeld.

The Hopewell ladies don't do that. We aren't at the Hamptons for the celebrities.

True, we may have stalked Ina Garten in the past, but never seriously. We never parked down the street from her house and sneaked through an open field, twisting an ankle in a groundhog hole, falling to the muddy ground, and totally ruining a very expensive pair of Frye boots.

We did go to the American Hotel every year to have a few drinks and a lovely lunch, but not just because Billy Joel was known to have lunch there as well. And we would never hang out across the street from the place in the pouring rain, watching the entrance, just because I overheard somebody mention that Billy had been seen down the street.

We saved the world-class restaurants for lunch, because we could save a lot of money that way and still get a great meal. Over the years, we'd eaten in most of the iconic eateries in the Hamptons. But our first meal each year, that very first lunch, was always at John Scott's Surf Shack.

The normal routine involved parking the car and heading out to the beach. We'd walk the eight-tenths of a mile down to the huge, white condominium complex, cut back to Dune Road, and then cross the street. John Scott's called itself a seafood shack. For a restaurant sitting on a piece of property worth more than the national debt of some developing countries, it looked just like that—a shack. The unpaved parking lot was surrounded by the kind of fence usually found around a corral, beer signs lit up the windows, and inside, fishing nets hung from the ceiling. Very non-world-class.

John Scott's had cold beer and lobster rolls, popcorn shrimp, and everyone's favorite, the Basket of Fries. Most of the patrons walked there from their multi-million-dollar homes, but everyone was friendly. And because it was so close to our rental house, we could drink as much as we liked because nobody had to be the designated driver. Although, in the past, we could have used a designated *walker*.

But since it was still raining when I finally turned onto Dune Road, we agreed to drive there instead. We went right past the mailbox of our beloved 461 and pulled into the restaurant's parking lot. I turned off the ignition. The heavy rain had stopped about a half hour ago, but it was misting. My shoulders and neck hurt from holding on to the steering wheel so tightly. I glanced back at Deb and Kelly.

"Should we wake her up?" I asked.

Tina had been asleep since Throgs Neck. We had talked around her, even talked about her, and she remained asleep, slumped forward in her seatbelt, making occasional snoring noises. Muffy had also napped, occasionally waking to snarl before repositioning herself on Tina's lap.

"I say we let her sleep it off," Deb said. "Even if it takes until Tuesday."

Kelly shook her head. "Deb, be nice. Of course we have to wake her up." She leaned forward to shake Tina's shoulder. "Time to wake up," she singsonged.

Tina made a small noise, much like a snort.

I leaned over and said very loudly in her ear, "Tina, we're here."

She did not wake up. But Muffy did, and she growled at me.

Deb opened the car door. "Let's leave her here. We can see the car from one of the tables by the windows. We can keep an eye on her. If she wakes up, we'll come and get her. Or we may get lucky and somebody will steal the van."

I desperately wanted to get out of the car, and it seemed like a perfectly logical plan. I cracked the window and opened the door to get out, stretching cautiously. The mist was fine but cold, and felt refreshing. Deb was doing minor calisthenics—squats and side bends.

"We weren't in the car that long," I told her.

"Yes, we were. Over three hours. I know this will aggravate my arthritis." Deb jogged in place for a few seconds, then headed for the front door of John Scott's.

It was the kind of place where everyone was a regular but us. We came in only once or twice during our stay, so we never expected the barman to look up and personally welcome us back, but I always kind of hoped that, just once, he would, like whenever Norm came in to *Cheers*.

We huddled in a table by the window and reached for menus. It was an empty gesture because we always ordered the same thing—beer, lobster rolls, and the Basket of Fries. Since the "season" didn't officially start until the following week, there was no waitress. I was on the end, closest to the bar, so I got up to tell the bartender our order. There were a dozen or so people sitting at the bar—a few older-than-we-were women in khaki slacks and faded cotton sweaters, a few nontourist types in jeans and T-shirts, and a tall guy in jeans and a polo shirt. He had a fairly decent butt. It was amazing to me how many men didn't appreciate the power of well-fitting jeans.

I stood beside him and ordered. The beers came first, of course, in frosted mugs. I grabbed the handles.

"Do you drink them one at a time," a very deep and somewhat sexy voice said, "or do you sip a bit from each mug?"

I turned.

The tall guy had the most amazing green eyes I'd ever seen. He looked to be my age—anywhere over fifty—and had a strong, chiseled face, with deep creases around those gorgeous eyes and a dimple you could drown in.

Something happened.

I remembered in *The Godfather*, when Michael was off in Sicily and saw that beautiful young girl for the first time and got hit with a thunderbolt. I always scoffed at that. Every reasonable grown-up knows that there's no such thing as Love at First Sight.

But there may very well be *Lust* at First Sight.

He smiled. White teeth, slightly crooked. "I'm Andy."

I felt myself smile back. "Ann. And these really aren't just for me. Although I could probably drink all of them with no problem." I nodded to our table by the window. "But we do have a contest to see who can down the first mug the fastest, if you want to watch."

"Should I bet on you?" he asked, still smiling.

"Normally, yes. But today I'd put my money on the short one wearing the Scarlett Knights sweatshirt. Deb had a particularly hard trip out this year."

"This year?"

I nodded, torn. The beer was getting warm. And I knew how badly my friends needed a little somethin' somethin'. But here was an attractive man, who not only was my age but could speak in complete sentences and might even have a sense of humor. This was an opportunity I could not pass up.

"Let me deliver these, and if you like, I can tell you all about it."

His smile grew broader. "I'd like."

I hurried back to the table and set down the beers. I took a couple of deep breaths.

"He's wearing Docksides with no socks," Deb noted about my new acquaintance. "I wonder if he owns a boat or if he just lacks couth."

"He's very cute," Kelly said, sipping her beer delicately. "And wearing no socks is perfectly acceptable. You *are* going back to talk to him, aren't you?"

"Yes. Should I? I mean he's pretty hot, right?" I couldn't believe it. I had just met an attractive man. I'd walked in and—bam—there he was, just standing there. "But I don't know how to talk to men anymore. I just talk to eight-year-old boys. About Greek gods and Transformers. I don't think I've had a meaningful conversation with a grown man since the bug guy and I had our termite talk last winter."

Deb sighed. "Exactly. Thank God you got rid of your gray hair, Annie. You're looking pretty good. I think it's time for you to stop being so coy. Go over and be charming."

"How? What should I talk about?"

"Anything," Kelly said. "After all, you already broke the ice, right? Don't overthink. Just be yourself."

"Yep." I bravely clutched my beer and went back to the bar.

This time I sat on the stool next to him, wishing that "myself" was a six-foot-tall blonde food critic, or maybe a retired fashion model. Anything but a librarian from New Jersey. I also wished "myself" had bothered to look in the rearview mirror before I left the van. Was my hair crazy from the humidity? That was usually the case. The best haircut in the world couldn't solve that problem. Had I remembered to put lipstick on when I left the house? I couldn't remember the last time I'd actually done that, but going to the Hamptons usually rated a swipe or two. If I *had* remembered, was there any left, or had I chewed it all off during the Throgs Neck crossing? Should I open my jacket so he could check out my boobs?

I forced myself to end my internal monologue before the man fell asleep in the silence.

"Deb noticed your Docksides. She wants to know if you own a boat," I said, by way of starting the conversation with charm, sophistication, and style.

He chuckled. "Not everyone you meet in the Hamptons is rich enough to hang out all summer on their yacht. Some of us who live out here have real jobs. Me, for instance." In front of him sat the remains of lunch: an almost-eaten burger, a few stray fries, and a glass of either straight vodka or water. I was guessing water.

"Ah, so you're not a multibillionaire, just off your super yacht, out slumming?"

He shook his head. "Sadly, no. Not even a multi*million*aire."

I sighed. "Damn. And here I thought I was finally getting lucky." Here I was making small talk. *Amusing* small talk. I knew that once upon a time I'd had that skill, but I thought I'd lost it completely.

He raised his eyebrows. "That's still a possibility."

I laid my hand over the general area of my heart and channeled Scarlett O'Hara. "Why, dear sir, what kind of girl do you think I am?"

He laughed. "I was hoping for hot and loose, but I'd be happy with funny and a terrific smile."

Oh. My. And the amazing thing was, instead of my anxiety level rising, I was feeling more relaxed as we went along. "You really live here? You're not, say, some guy from Jersey here for a little R and R?"

He looked genuinely puzzled. "Why on earth would someone from Jersey come out here before it's officially summer?"

"Well," I explained, "once it's officially summer, someone from Jersey could never afford a house right on the beach."

"Gotcha. So," he glanced back at Deb and Kelly, who were trying very hard to not look like they were trying to read our lips, "is this a yearly thing? Getting away from the husbands and kids?"

"Exactly. Only, for me, no kids anymore. Or husband, for that matter."

"How interesting." He drained the last of his water—or vodka—and pushed his glass away. "Kids all grown and out of the house?"

"My daughter is married and in Boston. My son is a broker. Wall Street. You?"

He shook his head. "Nope. My wife kept waiting for the right time. Apparently, it came right after she remarried. I parent vicariously through my brothers' kids."

"How many brothers?"

"Four. I was the youngest."

I laughed. "Were you the treasured baby, or the brunt of every joke?"

He laughed with me. "Spoken like a true youngest child. I was treasured. Irish mothers are like that."

I drank my beer. Here was a nice guy—relaxed and confident. "So, what's your dating situation?" I asked. "Are you online?" Might as well brazen this out. Either we'd end up as an epic love story or we'd never see each other again.

He made a face. "I tried that. There are some pretty crazy ladies out there," he said.

I nodded. "Yes, I'm sure. Just as there are some pretty crazy men."

He turned sideways to face me, his elbow against the bar. "Maybe we could introduce them?"

I shrugged. "Surely you'd think they could search one another out."

"Well, maybe that's what we could do. Create a dating site for crazies only. Krazydates.net?"

"Or noncrazies only."

He smiled. "But that might be just you and me."

I smiled back. "That doesn't sound so bad."

He nodded, and his smile deepened until it reached his eyes, causing the fine lines around them to crinkle. "No, it doesn't."

The bartender slid our food onto the counter.

"That's my cue. I have to get going anyway." He pulled out his smartphone and scrolled through. I was thinking fast. Should I ask to meet him again. Here? For a drink? Dinner?

"How long are you staying?" he asked, still looking at his phone.

"A week." My voice cracked.

"Why don't you give me your number? I'd be happy to show you some of the local haunts." He glanced up. "If you're interested. One noncrazy to another?"

"Ah." Really? I couldn't remember my cell number? "Yes, but wait." I scrunched my eyes closed and thought real hard.

Got it.

He smiled again and entered the number into his phone. He slid off the stool. He really was very tall.

"So. I'll call."

I nodded. "That would be good. Great."

He waved casually at Kelly and Deb as he walked out.

I turned to the bartender. "Do you know him? I asked.

The kid shrugged. "Not by name. I don't think he lives on Dune Road, but he drops in pretty regularly."

I gathered up the food to carry it back to the table. Kelly and Deb were grinning like fools.

"So? Did he really take your number?" Kelly asked.

I nodded. I could not stop myself from smiling.

"Let's hope he's not a sociopath," Deb said.

That lunch was, without a doubt, the best-tasting meal I'd ever eaten.

The Jersey Shore smelled of salt and fish. I loved that smell—it was a sign that the ocean was somewhere close by. Here on Dune Road, there was a different smell. Not so much salt, and no fish at all. It smelled . . . clean. And rich. Really. As if the people who paid several million dollars for a house on the water didn't want their air to smell like a fish market, so the ocean obliged them.

The house on Dune Road was one of the old shingle-style houses that really rich people built in the 1920s. It stood on stilts, which is how it weathered all the storms that had swept the coast during the past century. It had been completely renovated, with soaring windows, an open floor plan, a wraparound deck, and showers so big you could walk into them and jog around a little. From the outside it was old-world. Inside, more Pottery Barn.

We walked up the long steps to the front door, entered the code on the keypad, and then went in. We'd been coming here so long that there was a familiar "I'm home" kind of feeling when we walked in. The furniture was overstuffed and covered in pale, almost white, cotton. The floors were white tile topped with faded rag rugs. All the wood was washed out, by age or design. There was a fireplace for cool nights, and there were four bedrooms and four bathrooms.

We made a few trips bringing up everything from the car, and were finally left with only one thing to bring in the house—Tina.

I shouted at her, Deb shook her, Muffy yapped incessantly, but the woman snored on. I finally grabbed the dog and threw the nasty beast out of the car, where she promptly peed. She ran back to me, wrapped her little legs around my calf, and proceeded to hump furiously. I nudge-kicked her away, and she sat, yapping some more.

Kelly took a deep breath. "Let me try something," she said, and took out her phone. She dialed and looked expectantly at Tina.

Tina's cell phone rang, and, sure enough, on the third round, she sat up abruptly and reached into her purse.

"Hello?" she said.

"We're here," Kelly said, and ended the call.

Tina looked around in surprise. "We're here? I must have been napping." She struggled out of her seatbelt, almost toppled over as she tried to walk in the sand in stilettos, then scooped up her dog. "I love this house," she said, and tottered up the stairs.

Once inside, I gave her the quick tour. We put her suitcases in one of the smaller bedrooms, one with twin beds, and she made a little bit of a face.

"I usually sleep in a bigger bed," she said pointedly.

"Us too," Deb said. "And since we did all the heavy lifting, we got to pick first."

Deb and I got the two rooms with queen-size beds, simply because last year we'd shared one of the rooms with the twin beds. I was upstairs and could look out the sliding glass door at the ocean.

We made our list and went to Stop & Shop. Well, Deb, Kelly, and I did. Tina needed a shower and wanted to change. We were back in a little over an hour, to find Tina smoking cigarettes out on the deck in the cold and damp.

We unpacked a few things, opened a bottle of wine, and then grabbed some red plastic cups from a kitchen cabinet. We went out to the beach, took off our shoes, and started toward the water. Muffy ran around, yowling at the waves. The water was freezing cold, of course, but we told Tina we had to stand there for a few seconds, for the sake of tradition.

I raised my plastic cup. "To the seventh annual ladies' week away," I yelled against the wind.

We drank, then scooted out of the water onto the dry sand.

It was cold. The wind was fierce. And it started raining again. We drank some more.

Kelly raised her cup. "And remember, what happens on Dune Road stays on Dune Road."

We all laughed. We always laughed.

"Maybe this year," Kelly shouted, "Ann will have something happen that we need to leave on Dune Road?"

"Ann? What is Annie going to do?" Tina asked.

"That's what you get for sleeping," Deb scolded. "Wait till we tell you."

Then we ran back to the house.

The best thing about old friends getting together is that no one raises an eyebrow if someone suggests a nap before dinner. And we all had been friends for a long time. Joe and I stumbled across Hopewell in 1990, after we realized a two-bedroom apartment and a family of four couldn't work any longer. We'd reached out into the vast unknown—that is, anything west of Bergen County—and found a suburban paradise, complete with a small private lake and an adjacent state park.

The new Reynolds homestead was a comfortable raised ranch, just perfect for our family, about halfway up a shady hill. We packed everything from our two-bedroom apartment in Bayonne and moved—in three long, miserable days during an August heat wave—into four-bedroom, two-bath, air-conditioned luxury. The following Monday, I went to register our daughter, Brianne, for kindergarten. On the way back, I stopped at the playground by the lake, where I spent an hour or two with Bree and my three-year-old son, Travis. There were lots of other kids there, which I thought was a good sign. There were also lots of moms there, which puzzled me a bit. Why weren't they at work?

Granted, I wasn't at work either. Joe and I had scraped together every penny we could to buy the new house, but we were so used to living on a shoestring that I could afford to stay home a few years, until Travis went to kindergarten. I thought I was the exception, though—the cost of living in this part of New Jersey was such that two incomes were the norm. What was going on here in Hopewell?

When I got back to the house, I poured myself some white wine and waited for Joe to come home.

I didn't pounce on him right away, but waited for him to put down his briefcase and step halfway into the kitchen.

"Joe, we've got to move."

He kissed me on the forehead. "We just did, Annie. And I'm never doing it again as long as I live."

"No, Joe, I mean it. We have to get out of here. Now."

He sighed patiently. "Why?"

"Because this is Stepford."

He sat down at the kitchen table and ran his hands through his hair. "What?"

"You know, that movie? The Stepford Wives? Well, that's what Hopewell is. We have to leave."

He sat back and closed his eyes. "I had a really long day, honey. I have no idea what you're talking about. How is this Stepford?"

"I talked to some other moms today. They're all happy."

Joe nodded as he opened his eyes. "Really?"

"Yes. And they all work part-time or stay home. And I think they bake."

"Oh, God, no. Bake? How could they?"

"I mean it, Joe. This one woman? Doesn't work at all. She's pregnant, really pregnant, with her first kid. She was still hanging out at the playground, and she had chocolate-chip cookies that were still warm from the oven."

"Ann, one of the reasons we moved here was that the prices in Hopewell were lower than anywhere else in the area. Maybe she doesn't work full-time because she doesn't have to."

"That's another thing, Joe. Our Realtor told us that this house was below market value. Why is everything cheaper here? I mean, don't you think that's really strange? There has to be a reason, right?"

"There are a couple of reasons. We have no mail delivery, and have to go to the post office to get our mail. We have to pay for garbage removal. And there's a yearly HOA fee for snow removal. Plus, there's the lake, which we also pay for as part of the HOA, even though you have to join the club and pay extra to use the beach." He loosened his tie. "Where are the kids?"

"Well, I also met the woman across the street. She has a girl Bree's age and a son Travis's age, so they're all playing over at her house."

He raised an eyebrow. "Aren't you afraid they'll come back as little robots?"

I rolled my eyes. "Joe, it was the *wives* that were turned into robots. Not the kids, don't you remember? Perfect, beautiful robots who cooked and cleaned and were über-housewives?"

Joe chuckled. "And you say that like it's a bad thing."

"Joe!"

"Sorry. So what's the robot across the street named?"

"Deb Esposito. She was also at the playground, with her kids and her dog, and was talking about getting all the moms together the first day of school for a potluck breakfast after the kids got on the bus. They do that *every* year. Can you imagine?"

"And does she bake too?"

He had me there. I cracked a smile.

Joe drew me onto his lap and gave me a hug. "Ann, we knew there would be a few adjustments. This is Morris County, where they do things a little differently. We're not in Bayonne anymore. There's potluck here."

"But they're so friendly," I grumbled.

"Like I said. We're not in Bayonne."

"And they all said I should join the lake next summer."

"Why not? What else are you going to do with the kids all day? Annie, relax. We're deep in the heart of suburbia. In three years, Travis goes to kindergarten, and you can go back to work. Then you can stop playing nice and return to your type A self."

But by the next year, I'd become good friends with Deb. Her best friend was Kelly, and that pregnant lady? Her name was Jen, and we would all sit on one or the other's back deck in the evenings, watching for deer and talking. I was beginning to feel like I was part of something.

During that first year, I walked to the post office every day and knew all the local gossip. I spent the summer by the lake, reading and drinking white wine out of plastic cups. Bree went into the first grade, and I began attending PTA meetings and bake sales. When Travis started school, I got a part-time job at the local library. I even learned to make chocolate-chip cookies.

I had become one of the Hopewell ladies. And I loved it. And the women who stayed home and baked grew into good friends and strong, amazing women. When our kids were old enough, we all traded in our spare time for a "second act" career, Kelly getting her Realtor's license and Deb going back to nursing full-time. This week was our reward, and we treasured the time together—even the time spent curled up on the cozy couches, sleeping lightly while the smell of roasted chicken filled the house.

Chapter Four

"Annie, what's the itinerary for our week?" Kelly asked. We had successfully demolished half the roasted chicken, all the rosemary potatoes, and an entire container of Rocky Road. Then we settled around the empty fireplace.

I looked around. "I don't have one."

Kelly tilted her head. "What?"

I cleared my throat. "I didn't plan an itinerary. I thought we'd, you know, wing it."

Deb looked at me over the top of her glasses. "Wing it? We haven't winged it in years. You plan, we follow. That's how it's done."

"I know. Look, we all have our favorite places. I looked up some newish spots we could investigate, but I thought that maybe this year we could loosen up a bit. Itinerary-wise, that is."

Kelly rolled her eyes. "God, you mean we'll have to figure out where to eat breakfast on our own?"

I grinned. "Exactly. Besides, I've met Andy. That already adds an element of, well, the unexpected. What if he falls madly in love with me and we elope by Wednesday? Or what if we find Jason Wilde, and he invites us to spend the week on his yacht? I think we need to be flexible."

Deb shook her head slowly. "Who are you, and what have you done with my dear friend Annie Reynolds?"

I stuck out my tongue at her.

Tina let out a long and happy sigh. "Do you really think Jason will invite me to his yacht?"

Kelly shrugged. "Isn't he supposed to be working on his television series? I don't think that would leave him with a lot of downtime. And what's with the *me*? We're in this together, Tina. I wouldn't mind a bit of yacht time."

Deb opened up her Kindle. "As long as he supplies plenty of food and beer, I'm in."

"He's probably one of those shallow types who care only about themselves," I said. "If he does invite us, Tina, I'll pass."

Kelly arched her perfect brow. "Well, I have no problem with water. I'm hoping for the yacht."

Tina made a face and we all laughed.

Really? A yacht? Who were we kidding?

When my cell phone rang at a little before eleven that night, I saw "Private Caller" on the screen. I never answer Private Callers. If they want to talk to me, they should at least have the courtesy of introducing themselves first.

But—I'd given my number to Andy. He said he would call. He looked like a man of his word.

"Hello?"

"It's Andy. Is this too late?"

I smiled. Well, maybe grinned. "No. I'm just getting ready for bed. But I'm in the middle of changing into jammies, and I haven't brushed my teeth. Can I call you back in, like, ten minutes?"

He chuckled. "Tell you what. I'll call you back in fifteen. That way, both of us can have clean teeth, okay?"

I clicked off the phone.

He'd called.

And he was calling back.

I had a sudden urge to spray perfume between my breasts and slip into a filmy black negligee. Sadly, I didn't own a black negligee, and if I had, I wouldn't have packed it for the Hamptons. So I settled for my nightshirt with the little owls, because nothing says blooming romance like tiny red birds.

When he called back, I was sitting up in bed, staring at the phone, wishing I hadn't spent the past few years avoiding conversations with strangers, especially strangers who were also men. I could have used the practice. But then we started talking, and he didn't feel like a stranger. In fact, after a while, he felt like an old friend.

"Favorite band?" I asked him.

"Beatles. I'm showing my age, I know, but I don't care."

"Me too. Beatles, I mean. First true love?"

"Beth Stillman. Second grade."

"Judson Thuerk. Fourth grade."

"Judson?"

"When you're nine, it's a very romantic name. What do you do for a living?"

He groaned. "Do I have to tell you right away? My job freaks some people out."

Okay, so maybe he was a mortician. Or a bouncer in a high-class strip club. Or a hunter of baby seals. I was dying to find out exactly what this mystery job was but decided pushy was not the way to go. "Then my job will remain top secret as well."

"Deal."

He was silent for a moment. "There are some great nature trails around here. Quiet. Beautiful. I'm in the office tomorrow. Would you like to go for a hike on Tuesday?"

My hand tightened around the phone. "That sounds great."

"Yeah. It does. So I'll talk to you soon."

We hung up. When was the last time I'd talked to anyone for that long? He got my jokes. He made me laugh. He didn't make fun of me when I talked about how new and unexpected situations made me queasy. All that, and he liked long walks? We were clearly made for each other. I went to sleep with visions of green eyes dancing in my head.

Monday morning wasn't sunny. It was cool and gray. But I didn't care.

"At least there's no rain," Kelly said. We were huddled on the deck eating a breakfast casserole Deb had made the night before—browned sausage, torn-up bread, frozen hash browns, and eggs. She stuck it in the oven first thing, and it baked while we chatted and made coffee.

Deb had insisted we eat outside. The ocean looked rough. I held my coffee mug in both hands for warmth.

"Why are you so happy?" Tina grumbled. "It's cold and cloudy, and I can't even see the ocean from here because of all the mist."

I sipped my coffee, trying to control my grin. "I talked to Andy last night."

Deb's head whipped around. "Andy from the bar Andy? He really called you? Perfect. You meet an attractive man, and he's pushy."

"He's not pushy," Kelly said brightly. "That's what happens when a man asks for your phone number. He calls. And he doesn't wait three days."

"He's really great," I said, trying not to gush.

"Great? You can tell that from one short phone call?" Deb said. "He's probably a psychopath."

"Well, the first phone call was kind of short—like, only two minutes. But then he called back a few minutes later, and we talked for a long time."

"Why did he have to call you back?" Deb asked. "Did he have to go somewhere his wife couldn't hear him?"

"No, Deb. He's divorced. No kids. Lives in a condo somewhere out here. He called me back so I could brush my teeth and put my pajamas on and get into bed, so I could be comfy when we were talking."

"How thoughtful," Tina said. "What about him? Was he in bed too?" She arched her eyebrows. "Any phone sex?"

"No," I said. "We just talked. A lot. We both hate hockey and love the Mets. We both love Italian food, and we both had the same first job—camp counselors. We're practically made for each other." I sipped my coffee. "He wants to take me hiking on Tuesday."

"What?" Tina squeaked. "Hiking? You'd go out into the woods all alone with a strange man?"

"He's not strange," I insisted. "In fact, he seems very normal."

"Those are the ones," Deb said in a low voice, "that you have to watch out for."

"Why?" I asked. "What are the seemingly very normal ones going to do?"

"Rape and murder you," Deb said calmly, "and leave your body to rot in a swamp. Why else would he want to take you hiking, for God's sake? What's wrong with coffee? Or dinner?"

"We both like the outdoors," I said.

"Still," Kelly said, "what kind of first date is a hike? He should be trying to impress you. At least with drinks in a nice bar. How impressive is a swamp?"

"I don't think there are any swamps out here anyway. The Hamptons seem like a very unswampy kind of place," Tina said.

"Swamp, marsh, whatever—it might take years to find your remains," Deb said.

I stared at her, then Kelly. "Are you guys serious? Aren't you the ones who said I should come out here and meet someone? What happened to have a fling? *Fun and excitement?*"

Deb and Kelly exchanged a look.

"I'm just concerned about a relative stranger who wants to get you all alone, miles from nowhere. Concerned, that's all," Kelly said.

"As we have every reason to be. Where did you meet him?" Deb asked slowly, wagging her finger at me. "In. A. Bar."

"Yeah, but he met *me* in a bar, and I'm not going to leave his body in the swamp. Or marsh. Or whatever," I said.

"But we know that you're not a crazed maniac," Deb explained patiently.

"Neither is he!"

"We can only hope." Kelly shook her head. "Seriously, would you let your daughter go *into the woods*, alone, with some strange man she met while picking up lobster rolls and beer?"

I closed my eyes and took a deep breath. "Then what do you all advise for a first date that would not place my life in immediate danger?"

"I want to go on the record," Tina said, "as being wholeheartedly in favor of Ann picking up as many men as she can. But you'd really go out with a man named Andy?"

"What's wrong with his name?"

"Nothing," Tina said. "But Ann and Andy? Do you want to spend the rest of your life as one half of 'Ann and Andy'?"

"I will not," I said, "set limits on my possible happiness based on a person's name."

"Then coffee," Tina said. "During the day. Early, so if things go well, you can have lunch together. But someplace very crowded, so if he makes an unusual suggestion, you can scream and people will be able to rescue you." She looked very smug. "I've been on lots of first dates. I'm practically an expert."

"And how are you at second dates?" Deb asked, trying not to grin.

Tina sniffed and ignored her.

"All right, then. How about a Southampton day?" Kelly asked. She was on her phone now, scrolling. "There's an Alex and Ani store in Southampton now."

"Southampton it is," I said.

"Can we go to Sag Harbor instead?" Tina asked. "Jason Wilde hangs out in Sag Harbor."

Deb shrugged. "Today? Sure. After all, Ann wants us to be flexible. We always give Sag Harbor a full day. It has lots to do and see. But if you really think that celebrities walk around there like regular people, you're wrong. We've never seen *anyone*, and believe me, we've looked."

"But can we go? I mean today?" Tina looked hopeful. "You're the driver, Annie. How about it?"

I nodded. "Sure. The traffic should be light. Maybe the sun will be shining over there. And there's that great fish place right on the docks. Remember, Deb?"

Deb grinned. "Yes. My God, the lobster salad was amazing. And there's that funky little thrift shop, although it never has anything in my size. Nobody out here is larger than a double-zero."

"And the American Hotel," Tina said. "I read that Jason likes to go there."

I nodded. "The American is always on our list, Tina. There's a great bartender there who works the day shift. His name is Roy, and he makes the best drinks you'll ever taste."

She smiled. "Good. And we can ask him about Jason."

You'd think that since we each had our own bathroom, it wouldn't take more than an hour to get ready, but it usually did. Each of us had long ago figured out our Hamptons look. When you were built like I was—think fire hydrant on legs—you were limited to what looked chic and what didn't. I stuck to khakis and jeans, linen shirts that disguised the fact that I had no waist (and that my chest and hips are about the same diameter), and comfy shoes. Deb dressed a step or two down, and

Kelly a step up, but we were of the same mind-set. We realized that we'd never look like anything but tourists, so we gave up trying to look like we belonged. The rich just wore clothes differently than the rest of the world. Simple fact of life.

Tina, apparently, had a different outlook.

She emerged from her bedroom wearing shocking pink pants that hung low on her narrow hips and were held up by a skinny black-studded belt. Her shirt was a button-down, in pale yellow-and-white stripes. Draped around her shoulders was a white cardigan. Completing the outfit were spiked booties that came up to her ankles but left her toes bare, several chunky gold chains around her neck and wrists, and Jackie O sunglasses. She looked like she came from a whole other planet.

Deb, in jeans, sneakers, and her favorite Rutgers marching-band sweatshirt, raised an eyebrow. "Aren't your feet going to hurt wearing those things?" she asked.

Tina raised her sunglasses to the top of her head. "Why? Will we be doing a lot of walking?"

Kelly cleared her throat. Because she had naturally blonde hair, a perfect smile, and a tall and still-willowy body, Kelly was as close as we usually got to Hampton-esque. "Well, yes, Tina. That's kind of what we do here. Walk around and visit the shops. What did you think?"

Tina frowned. "But we agreed to go to the American, didn't we?"

"Yes," I said slowly. "But just for a drink. It's not like we were going to sit at the bar all day."

"Oh," Tina said. She fiddled with one of her necklaces. "Well, would you mind if I did that? I mean, I'm really not interested in shopping. You all could leave me there while you go off on your excursions. How does that sound?"

Deb grabbed her purse off the kitchen island. "Sounds perfect. Let's go."

Tina closed her eyes as we crossed the bridge, and once we were on the other side, the clouds disappeared. It wasn't exactly warm, and

Tina had to actually put on her sweater, as opposed to using it just as an accessory, but it wasn't raining. We made it to Sag Harbor in a bit under an hour, then spent fifteen minutes trying to park. I was not one of those crazy people who would cruise around looking for The Perfect Parking Spot. It took me that long to find *any* spot. As it was, we were three blocks from the center of town.

Tina started complaining about her shoes the minute we hit Main Street, so we pointed her in the direction of the American Hotel and sent her on her way.

Sag Harbor wasn't like some of the other towns in the Hamptons. I could almost believe that real people lived there. Of course, it was clean, and the buildings were well cared for, and there were plenty of high-end things to look at. But there was a homeyness about Sag Harbor that I loved. You didn't feel like you had to dress up just to walk down the street.

We eventually found our way to the Dock House, a small place right on the water that had become a favorite. We ate lobster rolls and scallops and watched a young and well-built crew clean a yacht moored across the way.

"Look at that. He's polishing the railing," Deb said.

"They polish everything," Kelly said. "It's their job."

"The people who clean my house don't look like that," Deb said.

I propped my elbow on the counter and leaned my chin on the palm of my hand. "Do you see that? He's not even using a mop or anything. He's on his hands and knees, with a rag, washing the deck."

"Swabbing," Deb said. "Swabbing the deck. With no shirt on. My God, look at his chest. I feel like I'm watching porn."

I nodded. "How pathetic are we?" I murmured. "Drooling over hot guys, cleaning."

There was an older woman, probably close to seventy, sitting at the counter next to us. Her hair was a very expensive shade of ash blonde, and there were extremely large diamonds on most of her fingers. She cackled.

"Don't feel like that, dearie," she said. "This is the best view in town."

We finally made our way to the American Hotel. Tina was perched at the bar, talking to Roy, my favorite bartender in the world. Roy was a fixture at the American, and the very first time we went there, I asked for a whiskey sour. Roy mixed one and it had been, without a doubt, the best drink I'd ever had. Then, he wouldn't let me pay for it. He hadn't made one in such a long time, he said, that it had been his pleasure.

He didn't recognize us at first, but when we all sat at the bar and asked for three whiskey sours, he smiled.

"You're back!" he said. He was from New Zealand and wore thick, black hipster glasses.

"Yes, once again," Kelly said. "How are you, Roy? Have you had a good year?"

He was busy mixing, but smiled. "Excellent. And you ladies?"

Deb nodded. "Great, thanks." She turned to Tina. "You missed a fabulous lunch, Tina. Lobster rolls and grilled scallops, and half-naked young men, cleaning. Pretty much a perfect day."

Tina smiled, a little lopsided. She had a half-empty wineglass in front of her. "I had something, not to worry. Roy and I have had a great chat."

Roy looked modest as he poured drinks. We all clinked glasses, even Tina, and sat there, drinking in the quiet elegance. I glanced back into the lobby. There were a few people scattered about. One was drinking coffee and reading, and two gentlemen were talking quietly over something-on-the-rocks. Any one of them was probably worth more than any of us would make in three lifetimes. Since I was driving, I had only one drink, but Deb and Kelly had another, and Tina had some more wine, so it was late afternoon before we finally left. We found the car, turned it toward home, and started immediately talking about dinner.

Kelly suggested chowder to go, so I turned the car around to head back east toward Bostwick's Chowder House. We were discussing New England versus Manhattan when Tina abruptly changed the subject.

"Roy says that Jason Wilde stops in almost every night for a drink at the American," she said.

She was sitting in the back next to Kelly. I glanced over at Deb and saw her make a face.

"Oh?" Deb said. "I'm betting lots of people stop for a drink at the American."

"So, I was wondering if we could come back here tonight. You know, just to hang out," Tina said, very casually.

I glanced at Deb again, who'd closed her eyes.

"Tina," Kelly said carefully, "we hardly ever go out at night."

"Why the hell not?" Tina asked, her voice a little sharp.

"Well," Deb explained, "it's very expensive, for one thing. And we're usually tired. Like tonight? I'm looking at an early bedtime 'cause I usually don't walk around this much, and my old bones can't take it."

"You're kidding," Tina said, sounding a bit angry. "You are kidding, right? I remember the first year we were here, we were out at a different place every night."

"We were all younger then," I explained.

Deb looked at me a bit wickedly over the top of her glasses. "Just because you've met Andy doesn't mean you should sit back. Fun and excitement, remember? You were going to troll for men."

Kelly looked over at me and shrugged. "True. We did kind of say that."

"But tonight? Tina, if you want, you can take the car," I offered.

"No, please don't make me come out here alone. I'll never be able to drive over the bridge, for one thing, and at night I know I'll get lost. Please, guys. Come out here with me. I'll pay for all your drinks."

We were stopped at a light, and I glanced back at Kelly. She nodded.

"Why not? Let's be adventurous," she said.

"How about it, Deb?" I asked. "Are you in?"

Deb shook her head. "No, thanks. Go ahead without me. I've got six new books on my Kindle. I'm good. Besides, I hated hanging out at bars to pick up guys when I was single. That's why I married Ben. And that's the main reason I'll never divorce him."

"Okay, then. Kelly and I will go with you. But not too late, okay, Tina?" I said. "And this is it with the Jason Wilde hunt. I'm not tracking him anywhere else."

She was beaming. "Thank you. And I promise, I won't ask you to chase Jason Wilde again after tonight. I swear."

With everything else that happened, we all later agreed that she *had* kept her word.

I stopped at a farm stand for fresh salad fixings and a cherry pie to go with the chowder, and we ate at the long table that sat between the living room and kitchen. By about 6:30 I was full, happy, and pretty much ready to crawl into a corner of the couch. That's when Tina announced that she was going to start to get ready.

"For what?" Deb asked.

"The American Hotel, silly." Tina rolled her eyes. "You can't expect me to go out there dressed like this, do you?"

"It was good enough for earlier today," Kelly pointed out.

"I know," Tina said. "But I imagine it's a much different crowd at night." She went off to her room. Kelly and I looked at each other.

"Should we change too?" Kelly asked.

I shrugged. "Into what? She's probably going to come out in a designer something and six-inch heels. My best outfit is a five-year-old linen sundress and Birkenstocks."

Kelly looked thoughtful. "Well, I've got black leggings, that olive-green tunic, and ballet flats. Maybe I'll put my hair up. What do you think?"

Kelly would look classy and beautiful in flannel pajamas and pig-tails. Deb and I both nodded.

"What about me?" I asked.

Deb got up off her chair. "Ann, you used to have great clothes. What happened to you? Have you at least got a pair of khakis? I bought that cotton sweater thing from the consignment shop today for Natasha. It should fit you just fine. And, it's froufrou enough for An Evening at the American." She made elaborate hand gestures and shook her head. "Let's try it on."

"But you just bought it, Deb," I said, following her. "Won't your daughter be upset if somebody else wears it first?"

"Annie, it's from a *consignment* shop. It's a given that somebody else wore it first, remember?" Deb said. "Consider it a sacrifice for the cause."

Her bedroom was directly below mine, and had the same layout, but it looked like her suitcase had exploded all over the room. I glanced around.

"Ah, Deb, we've only been here twenty-four hours."

She chuckled. "So I should worry about the neat police? Let's see if I can find—here it is." She dug under three sweatshirts, found a paper shopping bag, and then pulled out the sweater. It was quite nice, a long tunic in pretty shades of blue and green.

I held it up. "Good for celeb stalking?"

Deb nodded. "Very classy. No one will ever suspect you. Take this necklace and put on dangly earrings. You'll look great."

I took it upstairs to change, then met Kelly on the landing. She was wearing a silk tunic that floated gracefully over her body, and her blonde hair was swept up, with a few wispy curls around her face. As always, Kelly looked poised and sophisticated.

"I'm ready to meet Cary Grant. What do you think?" she asked, twirling gracefully on her toes.

It was hard not to be jealous of Kelly. She did not look her age. Her skin glowed, no gray peeked through in her honey-blonde hair, and her boobs didn't sag. Her children were equally gorgeous, as well as smart, and did things like volunteer at soup kitchens and graduate from Dartmouth. None of us could figure out why her husband had suddenly left her, especially as there was no Other Woman lurking in the background. Kelly once hinted at an Other Man, but she didn't elaborate, and we never pressed.

She had always wanted to be an interior designer, and with her innate flair for style, it was a good fit. But, she explained, it was easier to get a real-estate license than an ASID certification. So she became a Realtor, and a very successful one, because she could walk into any house and make her clients see all the possibilities. She even carried paint samples in her tote bag. She was a natural.

I nodded. "You look great. With your hair up like that, and that necklace, you look like a native."

Kelly grinned, and we went downstairs to wait for Tina.

And waited.

Kelly and Deb had a glass of wine, and Kelly watched MSNBC while Deb and I talked about creating our own reality-TV show, The Real Housewives of Hopewell. Kelly had another glass of wine, and we all started watching Law & Order reruns. I was curling up in the corner of the couch and letting my eyes close when Tina whirled into the room in a rush.

"Okay, I'm ready. Let's go," she said.

Kelly and Deb and I stared at her.

Tina's maroon hair was brushed straight up to a small peak at the top of her head. She was wearing a formfitting red dress that was roughly twenty-seven inches long from the tops of her barely-there breasts to the bottom of her mostly flat butt. Her legs were bronzed, and the heels added six inches to her height. Her gold hoop earrings looked to weigh four pounds each. In her hand was a glittery clutch.

Tina looked around, smiling. "Do I look amazing?"

"What?" I asked.

"Are you kidding?" Kelly blurted out.

"Too much?" Tina asked with a frown.

Deb laughed. "For what? If you're planning to hang out in a hotel lobby somewhere with a FOR RENT sign around your neck, you're perfect."

Tina turned on her spiked heels and went back into her bedroom.

I went back to the television, Kelly called her daughter and had a fight with her about the upcoming Memorial Day weekend, and Deb fell asleep. Tina emerged again, this time in a black skirt that looked like a ballerina's tutu, a gold sweater that fell off one boney shoulder, and gladiator sandals.

"Better?" she asked brightly.

"Great," I said, jumping off the couch.

"You look amazing," Kelly enthused.

Deb opened one eye, yawned, and nodded. "Very chichi."

We got to the American just after nine. Tina immediately went up to the bartender to ask if Jason had been in yet, then reported back that Jason hadn't yet made an appearance, and we could just sit and wait.

Rather than perch on the bar stools, we settled into a few empty chairs in the lobby. Tina bought the first round and we sat, chatting quietly. The dinner crowd had thinned, and the restaurant was practically empty. Tina kept watching the front door while Kelly and I amused ourselves by making up life stories of the various people who passed us in the lobby.

"She's the heiress to a billion-dollar fortune," I said, nodding to a tiny hunched-back lady with white hair, clutching the arm of a very good-looking man in his sixties. "She's leaving all her money to her caregiver, whose name is Carlos. They used to be lovers years ago, and now he's the only one she speaks to. I bet if you went over and struck up a conversation with Carlos, you might end up a very rich wife."

Kelly shook her head. "Carlos is gay and has been dallying around with the pool boy for years," she said in a low voice. "You know that nothing like that ever happens to me."

I nudged Kelly's shoulder. "That's because you haven't found anyone good enough. Now see this one? Who looks like a rich, retired archaeology professor? I bet he'd be thrilled to have you buy him a drink."

Kelly rolled her eyes. "He probably has twelve cats," she said, and we both laughed.

Tina suddenly sprang to attention. "He's here," she hissed, shrugging her shoulders, causing the sweater to slip down a little farther.

We all looked toward the front door. Jason Wilde may have had questionable acting skills, but, boy, could he make an entrance.

He had pushed open the door and was standing there, the street-light behind him surrounding him in a halo. He swept his hand through his hair, then shook his head, his eyes moving right past where we were sitting and sweeping to the back of the bar. He was obviously look-ing for the perfect spot to spend the evening, and considering that he barely paused when he saw us, I figured that we weren't going to be a consideration.

But I hadn't counted on Tina. She suddenly shifted in her seat and crossed her legs, and a whole lot of thigh burst into view.

She waved a hand. "Jason? Jason Wilde? Is that really you?"

He stopped midway across the lobby and turned to her. "Hey. Yes. It's really me. Do I know you?"

Tina shook her head. "No. I'm Tina." She held out her hand, and he reached down to shake it. "I'm a huge fan. We all are," she said, nodding to Kelly and me. "Would you like to sit? We could make some room."

Jason looked back at the entire restaurant again. The bar area was deserted. There were mostly empty tables in the dining room. The cold and the fog had kept most people in their very expensive homes.

"Sure, Tina. That sounds fun." And he sat down.

Jason Wilde was dressed in jeans, a pink button-down shirt, and an expensive-looking black-leather jacket. He was smaller than he looked on television—barely five eight—and slender. I knew he had to be on the down side of forty, but aside from a few crinkles around the eyes, he looked much younger. In fact, he was gorgeous. Thick golden hair, piercing blue eyes, and perfect teeth in a dazzling smile.

I was shocked. I could not believe that Jason Wilde had even showed up. Not only that, but instead of running like hell from Tina's less-than-subtle approach, he had actually smiled and sat down. Kelly's face lit up. I didn't want to stare, but, gosh, I couldn't look away.

Jason looked at Kelly. "I'm Jason," he said, and held out a hand.

Kelly took it and held it for a moment, smiling brilliantly. She was starstruck. "Of course you are. I'm Kelly. And this is Ann. Great to meet you. Can we buy you a drink?"

He looked sheepish. "My doctor is trying something new for my back. I hurt it—"

"While filming the promo for your show last fall," Tina finished, a little breathlessly.

He nodded. "Yeah. It was starting to bother me again, and I've got this new patch thing. I'm not supposed to be drinking," he said.

"And yet, here you are," Tina said, "sitting with us in a bar. Just one round?"

Jason shrugged. He was looking at Tina somewhat cautiously. I'm sure crazed fans approached him all the time, and he was probably sizing up the risk-reward factor. "Sure," he said finally.

Kelly waved to the bartender. "Another round," she called out. "And . . ." She looked at Jason, who shrugged and said loudly, "The usual."

He was sitting between Kelly and Tina. "So, ladies, what brings you to Sag Harbor?"

Tina opened her mouth, but Kelly beat her to it by a fraction of a second. "We come out every year. Girls' week away, you know?"

Jason nodded, his eyes moving slowly from Kelly's smooth, golden hair down to her thin, also-golden anklet. "Great. So are any of you married?"

This time Tina was ready. "I'm not," she said breathlessly.

The bartender came by with drinks. Kelly dropped some cash on the tray. Tina grabbed her drink, then leaned forward toward Jason. "Here's to meeting you at last," she purred.

Jason clicked her glass, and then made sure he toasted Kelly and me as well. He sipped thoughtfully, looking at us, probably trying to figure out what the hell we were doing here in the first place.

"So, is the American one of your hotspots?" he asked.

Tina nodded. "Yes. Why, we're practically regulars."

I started choking on my ginger ale, and Kelly thoughtfully patted me on the back.

"It's a little slow around here right now," Jason said. Whatever he was drinking was gone in three long gulps.

Tina glanced around. "Yes, but it's so much better than fighting all the crowds. Besides, I'm usually too busy during the summer to get away."

Jason leaned back in his chair and nodded his head. "Really? And what do you do?"

Kelly and I both sat up. Tina had always been a little vague about her job, but apparently Jason deserved the truth, the whole truth, and maybe a bit more than the truth.

"I'm the assistant to the vice president of a small investment company. Mostly we deal in short-term, high-return properties, usually bought for tax reasons. If you're ever looking to hide a bit of money in, say, a small, exclusive resort in Malaysia, I'm the person to talk to."

He looked at her as though she tested spacesuits by making regular trips to Jupiter. "Really? That sounds amazing. High finance is completely foreign to me. I have people who take care of my money for me, or I'd have been living on the street years ago." He turned and fixed his gaze on Kelly. "So, Kelly, what is it that you do?"

Kelly, I could tell, was getting the most out of her moment in the spotlight. "Real estate," she said. She leaned forward and lowered her voice, as though sharing a great secret. "Residential."

"Tough gig," Jason observed.

She shrugged. "Yes, well . . ."

"I bet you're very good at it," Jason went on. "I can tell. I'm really good about reading people. You're very beautiful, and I'm sure that helps, but it takes more than that. It takes good instincts and lots of patience. And I bet you have to be able to figure out what your client really needs, not just what they want. Am I right?"

Kelly's jaw dropped slightly. So did mine. I knew that she always worried about her looks getting in the way of being taken seriously. She also told me the hardest part of her job was figuring out what a person really needed in a home, not just what they wanted.

How did Jason know?

Then it was my turn. "And you?"

"I work in a library. In the children's department," I said, half expecting him to follow up with an observation about diversity in children's literature or the rise of the dystopian YA novel.

He looked fascinated. "I bet you have a blast. I don't read much anymore. Not for fun, anyway. After looking at scripts all day, my eyes need lots of rest. But I loved reading as a kid. He leaned in and dropped his voice. "I wanted to be a Hardy Boy." He sat back and looked down at his empty glass, then signaled the bartender. "Shots all around. Wild Turkey. On my tab."

"I can't," I said. "I'm the driver." I held up my glass. "Ginger ale."

Jason made clucking noises. "Too bad. You look like the type of lady who loosens up pret-ty nice."

The old, battered feminist part of me reared its head in anger and defiance. How dare he? The wistful, gosh-I'd-like-to-date-again part of me silently jumped up and down and squealed. Torn, I just smiled.

Boy, this guy oozed charm. More than that, he had The Gift. I'd seen it before, and it was hard to resist. When he spoke to you, you felt like the most important person in the room.

He stretched out his foot and nudged Kelly's leg. "Kelly here will have a shot with me, right?"

"Ah . . ."

I glanced over at Tina. She had a strange look on her face. She was the one who was the Jason Wilde fan, and he was not reacting to her the way she'd hoped. She was obviously fighting an intense battle between wanting to murder Kelly and me, and wanting to ask us what we were doing to get his attention that she wasn't.

The answer to that was obvious. We weren't trying all that hard.

She, on the other hand, was transparently obsessed.

The bartender arrived. The shot glasses gleamed almost golden in the lamplight. Jason raised his glass and downed it quickly. Then he grabbed another. And looked at me.

"This has your name on it. You sure?"

I nodded. He drank it down.

If this was what he was like when he wasn't supposed to be drinking, I couldn't imagine him in full swing.

"How's the show doing?" I asked him.

His face lit up. "It's going great. Really. We were worried about getting picked up again, but this season is going to be amazing. I mean, it's the Hamptons, right? Everybody wants to see what life is like among the super-rich."

"And what is life like?" Kelly asked.

He shrugged. "Well, I can't tell you firsthand. I mean, these people out here? Lots of money. More than I'll ever see."

Tina was reining herself in but couldn't help her body language. She leaned forward, recrossed her legs, and fluttered her fingers at him. "What? A big television star like you?"

He shrugged again. "I'm not that big. Otherwise, I'd be looking at 'short-term, high-return' properties." He smiled at her, a "See, I was listening" kind of smile that, I could tell, went a long way. "And audiences are fickle. I mean, one day you're riding high and *Entertainment Tonight* wants to do a profile, and the next day you're out doing regional theater."

Tina made a choking sound and paled slightly.

Jason didn't notice. He leaned forward, his eyes bright. "I'd done a series before, you know," he said, in a just-between-us kind of tone.

"I loved that show," I gushed.

He rewarded me with a look that told me I'd said exactly the right thing. "Thanks. I had a blast. It took me a while to find the perfect series to do again. You have to be very careful about career choices, you know."

We all nodded, none of us mentioning those career choices that allowed anyone with the price of a ticket to see his wanker on the giant screen, not to mention in the privacy afforded by a flat screen and a DVR.

"How long have you been doing yoga?" Tina asked.

He frowned. "Yoga?"

Tina slithered a little closer. In fact, she was at the absolute edge of her chair. Her very next move would land her directly in his lap. "Yoga. You know, like on the show." She dropped her voice so she had to lean in just a little bit more, giving him the opportunity to look directly down the front of her gold sweater if he chose.

He did not take advantage. In fact, he backed off just a bit. "I don't know anything about yoga," he said. "I just do as I'm told."

"Well," Tina breathed, "that just shows what an amazing actor you are. I thought you'd been doing it for years."

A very odd expression came over his face. "Doing what?"

Tina frowned slightly. "Yoga."

He appeared to be listening to Tina. Very hard. "Yoga?"

Her patience never wavered. "Yes. In the show?"

His eyes narrowed even further. "Show? What show?"

Tina laid a concerned hand on his thigh, just four inches above his knee.

"Are you okay?" she asked.

He wet his lips with the tip of his tongue. "What show?" he asked again. Very, very slowly.

Kelly cleared her throat. "Ah, Jason? Are you okay? Jason? It looks like your medication just met the Wild Turkey."

He leaned forward, and as he did, he practically fell off his chair. "Naw, I'm great. I just don't know about this show you're talking about." He glanced around and dropped his voice to a whisper. "Are we on camera now?"

"I think someone's drunk," I said. "How did you get here, Jason? A cab? Are you staying in Sag Harbor?"

He shook his head and turned in my direction, squinting. "I drove."

Kelly's shoulders slumped. "Well, you can't drive back. Where are you staying?"

Jason frowned. You could almost hear his brain creaking. "I have a house. Dune Road."

Tina lit up. "That's where we're staying. We can take you home!"

What did she just say? Take him home? In my car? I did not want a drunken television star in my car.

Kelly looked sternly at Tina. "We can call him a cab."

Tina shook her head. "No. We owe him. After all, we got him drunk."

Kelly made a noise. "It's not our fault he's a lightweight," she muttered.

"Jason," Tina asked him slowly, "would you like us to take you home?"

He licked his lips. "Tha' be great," he said with much difficulty.

Tina looked at me with puppy-dog eyes.

I shook my head. "I do not want to be responsible for this drunk actor. What if something happens?"

If Tina had been Muffy, she'd have been dancing in circles on her hind legs, tail waving frantically. "Ann, come on. Kelly, tell her. It will be fine."

Kelly sighed in surrender. "Annie, we're giving the guy a lift, that's all. How much worse can he get?"

I sighed. "Okay, I guess. We can take him home. No big deal."

He stood up slowly, one hand on Tina's shoulder, and they walked out first. Kelly rolled her eyes as we followed them out of the American and into the chilly night.

Chapter Five

I really didn't expect Jason to be too much of a conversationalist. After all, he was drunk and might be a little embarrassed by the whole situation. So I just drove, humming along to the radio. We were halfway across the bridge before I said anything to him.

"So, Jason, where are we taking you?" I asked.

Silence.

"Ah, Jason?"

"I think he passed out," Tina said nervously. "He kind of fell against me awhile back, and he's snoring."

"Well, how are we supposed to take him home if he's passed out?" I asked, feeling annoyed. "I knew this was a mistake. Now what do we do?"

Kelly turned around and looked in the backseat. "Tina, see if you can get out his wallet. If we're lucky, he's got a New York license with an address on it."

Go Kelly.

Tina must have been having a field day back there, moving her hands in and out of his pockets, but she finally handed a wallet to Kelly, who opened it up, then turned on the interior light.

"Well, poop," she said.

"Doesn't he have a license?" I asked.

"Yes. For California." I glanced over. She was pulling out bits of paper. "Nothing with a New York address. God, he's at the ATM a lot. Look at all these friggin' receipts!"

"What do we do with him?" I wailed. "How did this happen?"

Remember that contented rut I told you I was in? This was exactly the kind of thing that really threw a wrench into things. True, I'd met a man, and might even see him again, and *that* was certainly a ripple in my quiet little life. But I'd met a man before. I kind of knew the script. But this? A semifamous actor, passed out in the backseat of my minivan? What the heck was I supposed to do with that? With him?

"I guess," Tina said in a small voice, "we'll just have to take him home with us."

I clenched my teeth and drove in silence. Turning into the drive at 461 Dune Road, I slammed the minivan into park and took a cleansing breath. This was really no one's fault, I told myself. Just absurd bad luck.

Tina opened the back door, then jumped out. Kelly and I also got out, and we all peered into the backseat.

Jason Wilde was slumped over, snoring very loudly.

"I still can't wake him up," Tina said a little nervously.

"Perfect," Kelly said. "We can't let him sleep all night in the car. He might freeze to death."

She had a point. It was not what you'd call seasonable. In fact, it was downright cold, and the wind off the water was fierce.

"We could bring him inside," Tina said. "He's much smaller than he looks on TV. I bet the three of us could carry him."

So she scooted back in, unlatched his seat belt, then started pulling at his arms. Kelly opened the door on the other side of the minivan to push. I grabbed his shoulders as he slid out, and Tina and I lowered him onto the sand.

"This is a good start," Tina said brightly.

Kelly had come around. She helped drag him away from the van. Tina shut all the doors. Kelly and I each took one of his arms, draped them around our shoulders, and Tina reached for his legs.

"One, two, three . . . go," I said.

We all scurried around the van, against the wind, over to the foot of the stairs. The stairs weren't wide enough for Kelly and me on either side of him, so we eased him down, then each of us grabbed an arm, trying to bring him up the stairs. It was not going well.

Tina dropped his feet. She was breathing like a winded racehorse. "I need a sec," she gasped.

Kelly looked worried. "Should I get Deb?"

I nodded. Kelly dropped Jason's arm and ran up the stairs. I eased down onto a step. Jason's head was against my knee, and he smelled of bourbon.

"Lightweight," I muttered. Really, the guy had a few shots and was practically comatose. Whatever medication he was on that wasn't supposed to mix with alcohol needed to issue a stronger warning. I sat there for five minutes (but what seemed like at least an hour) before I heard the door above open.

"What in the hell have you done?" Deb yelled.

"Shush!" I yelled back.

Deb came down the steps. "There's nobody around. Who is that? Is he dead?"

"Jason Wilde. He passed out," I explained.

"On our stairs?"

"No, Deb, in the car. We were supposed to be giving him a ride home." I said. "For the record, I was against it." I struggled to stand up, and Jason's head thunked lightly against the step. "We're trying to get him inside."

Deb was shaking her head. Kelly was standing behind her, looking worried in the glow from the porch light.

Deb took a deep breath. "The stairs are just barely wide enough for two people. We need to roll him on his side, each of us grab a piece of him, and see if we can get him up to the top without breaking anything."

I eased down a few steps, and Deb came down next to me.

"Okay," Deb said, "see if we can get him on his side."

I reached under him, found the back pocket of his jeans, took hold, and we all pushed. He rolled over onto his left side, the front of his body propped against the wall of the house.

"Good," Deb said. "Now, everybody reach under him and grab something, and we'll all lift him together. Don't rush. We can go up one step at a time. God, if we drop him, he'll probably be brain damaged, so be careful."

I reached around him again and clasped my arms around his, well, let's say upper thighs. Tina had his feet. Deb was holding his stomach, and Kelly brought her arms under his armpits, her hands clasped against his chest.

"Let's go," Deb said. "And be careful. If I break a nail, I'm going to be pissed."

We all went up one step. He really wasn't that heavy. Then, another step, and another. It took us less than a minute to get him up the stairs, across the porch, and through the open door into the kitchen.

"Now where?" Kelly asked.

"My room," Tina said.

We all looked at her.

"It makes sense," she said, looking perfectly innocent and sounding surprisingly logical. "I'm on the first floor, and I have twin beds. Do we really want him on the couch?"

She had a point, so we shuffled around the corner, into the bedroom, swung him around, then dropped him onto the bed. Muffy raced in from somewhere, jumped on the bed—quite an impressive feat for such a tiny dog—and growled softly while sniffing Jason's butt.

He lay still as a stone, snoring softly, one arm dangling to the floor. We all stared at him, and he emitted a long, loud fart. Muffy backed away, whining.

"Well, that's certainly impressive," Deb muttered. "I can finally take *meeting an unconscious actor* off my bucket list."

I went into the kitchen, found the tequila, and took a small sip, right from the bottle. I told Deb what happened, Kelly added her bit (and took a couple of sips as well) and then we all looked around for Tina. Who was still, apparently, in her bedroom with the unconscious actor.

"Tina," Deb barked, "get out here, would ya?"

Tina came out, looking breathless and happy. "I got his jacket, shirt, shoes, and socks off," she said. "Can one of you help me with his pants?"

"No!" Kelly and I said together.

"You cannot be undressing that man," Deb said between clenched teeth. "Are you crazy? Or is that your usual method of getting a man naked?"

Tina looked defensive. "There's nothing wrong with wanting him to be comfortable."

"Maybe not," Deb shot back. "But there's everything wrong with you stripping him down to his skivvies."

Deb turned and marched back into Tina's room. We all followed.

"So this is James Wind?" Deb asked.

"Jason Wilde," Tina explained. "He starred in a very successful television show back in 1998 as a private detective with a talking schnauzer. Then he made a few movies."

Deb was looking at his face, well, his profile at least. "Was he in that thing about the alien invasion and the rock star, where he dropped trou every five minutes?"

"Yes," Tina said excitedly. "He was nominated for a Golden Globe for that one."

Deb shook her head. "Well, at least I know why you wanted to get his pants off."

He was still lying on his stomach. Muffy was curled up next to him on the bed, looking happy for the very first time. Deb reached over delicately to slide her hand into the back pocket of his jeans, easing out his cell phone. She swiped the screen a few times, then dropped the phone on the bed in disgust. "It's locked."

"Who were you trying to call?" Kelly asked. Good question.

"Anybody who can get him out of here. Doesn't he have a girl-friend? Or boyfriend?" Deb asked.

Tina nodded. "Tasha Montgomery. She's a singer. Tasha is also the star of—"

Deb held up a hand to cut her off. "I don't care who she is, Tina. But the poor thing is probably going to wonder where the hell her boyfriend is."

Tina made a face. "I doubt it. I mean, they're living together, and she's supposed to be out here with him, but rumor has it they're not getting along too well these days."

"Maybe we should call the police," Kelly suggested. "Just to tell them that he's here. That way, if this Tasha person—"

"No," Tina yelped. She glanced at all of us and cleared her throat. "No, we can't call the police."

"And why not?" I asked.

She cleared her throat again. "Because, legally speaking, I'm not supposed to be within seventy-five yards of him, that's why."

Kelly closed her eyes.

Oh, dear.

We were back out on the deck. The night was cold and starless, and the ocean sounded far away. Tina and Kelly were both smoking cigarettes;

and Deb had thoughtfully brought out the tequila, along with lemons, salt, and shot glasses, all on a cute flamingo-shaped tray. We all did a proper shot in silence. Then Deb licked the last bit of salt off her lips.

"So tell us," she said to Tina. "And this damn well better be good."

Tina poured herself a little more. "Well, do you remember that crack he made about regional theater? He actually starred in *Present Laughter* at the Paper Mill Playhouse a few years ago. Did you see him?"

We shook our heads. She rolled her eyes in obvious amazement.

"Well, it ran for one month, and I had tickets for all the performances." She sprinkled a little salt on her hand and took another shot.

Deb stared. "You saw every performance for the entire month?" she asked.

Tina shook her head. "No. I had tickets for all of them, but I couldn't go to any of them after the first two weeks because of the restraining order."

Kelly reached for the bottle. "The Paper Mill Playhouse had a restraining order against you?"

"No," Tina said. "Jason did."

"Holy crap," Deb muttered. "You're practically a felon."

"Why would he do that?" I asked.

Tina shrugged. "He claimed I was stalking him."

Deb wrestled the tequila out of Kelly's hands. "Holy crap," she said again.

"Well, were you?" I asked.

She shrugged again. "If he had only agreed to have dinner with me the first time I asked, I wouldn't have sent him all those e-mails. Or made any phone calls. And I *never* would have waited for him at the stage door. He should be more gracious to his fans."

Kelly frowned. "How did you get his phone number in the first place?"

"I bribed one of the backstage people. They borrowed his cell during a performance and called me from it so I could capture his number."

Tina made a face. "I don't know why it became such a big deal, but it did. And as far as I know, the restraining order still stands."

"But he didn't recognize you at the bar," I said, confused.

"Well," Tina explained, "my hair was long and blonde then, and I hadn't had any work done. Even you said I looked like a different person."

Deb ran her hands through her short hair, tugging at the ends. leaving it standing straight up and looking a little scary. "Which means you can also be arrested for trying to impersonate a normal person. Well, I guess we can let him sleep it off, and hopefully he still won't recognize Tina in the morning." She pointed her finger at Tina. "Don't take any more of his clothes off," she ordered.

Tina shook her head. "I won't. I won't even touch him. I'll just lie there and watch him sleep."

"Yeah, whatever," Deb said. "It's freezing out here. I think I have frostbite on my little toe. Let's go to bed."

I went inside, helped with the quick cleanup, and then headed upstairs with Kelly. I followed her into her bedroom.

"Do you think we'll get into trouble?" I asked her.

She shook her head. "I doubt it. He was drunk, so drunk that he passed out. He'll probably be so embarrassed when he wakes up, he'll never tell a soul."

I hugged myself. "I just have a bad feeling about this, that's all."

"Don't worry. What's the worst that could happen? He'll wake up grumpy and pissed off. So what?"

"Yeah, you're right." I shuddered. "'night."

"Good night."

As I crawled into bed, I checked my phone. It was almost eleven. As I stared, it pinged. A text from Andy.

Are u awake?

I called him back. "I'm just getting into bed," I said.

He chuckled. "What a tease. How was your night? Any crazies try to sweep you off your feet?"

"As a matter of fact, I was flirted with. Outrageously. By a younger man."

"Wow, you Jersey girls know where the action is."

"I'm not sure he was very sincere," I said.

"Well, know that when I flirt with you, it will be very sincere."

I felt myself blushing. "And when exactly were you planning on doing this flirting?"

"I'm an excellent multitasker. I can hike, lecture on the natural wonders of Long Island, and be incredibly charming, all at the same time."

"Wow. And here I thought I'd just be getting sand in my shoes."

"Be prepared. I'll see you tomorrow?"

I sighed happily. "You bet."

I had left the sliding door in my bedroom open just a little bit the night before so I could go to sleep listening to the sound of the ocean. I hadn't counted on a cold front slamming into Long Island. When I woke up the next morning, it was cold. Really cold.

I got out of bed to shut the sliding glass door. There was a wall of fog outside so dense I couldn't see the ocean. I ran to the bathroom, then jumped back in bed and snuggled under the covers, thinking I could get at least another half hour of sleep.

"Annie, are you awake?"

It was Tina.

"Yeah. What's up?"

She looked nervous. "Jason won't wake up."

I sat up in bed. "What do you mean, 'won't wake up'?"

She stared at the floor. "I tried to wake him up, you know, to, ah, make him coffee. And he won't open his eyes.

I could imagine why Tina wanted him awake, and I was pretty sure coffee had nothing to do with it, but still. "I'll be down there is a second."

She left, and I traded my pajama pants for jeans. I yelled for Kelly and headed downstairs. I knocked on Deb's door. "You awake?"

"Sure. Come in."

She was propped up in bed, watching the news. "What's up?"

"Tina says Jason won't wake up."

She threw off the covers. "I have to pee. Give me a sec."

Tina was sitting on the edge of her bed. Muffy was curled up around Jason's head, and she bared her teeth at me.

I shook Jason by the shoulder, and Muffy snapped at me. I jumped back.

"Tina," I said loudly, "do something with this dog before I stuff her in a pillowcase and throw her in a closet."

Tina swooped the dog up, then carried her to the sliding glass door that opened to the deck. She tossed Muffy out, calling sweetly, "Make wee-wee for Mommy. That's a good girl."

I shook Jason again. "Hey, Jason, rise and shine."

He made a snorting, snuffling kind of noise.

"Wake up!"

Tina came over and stood on his other side. "See?"

"Hey, Jason!" I yelled in his ear. I shook him, hard, for almost thirty seconds. No response.

Kelly had come in behind me. "Can he still be drunk?"

"He didn't have that much to drink," I said. "Maybe it's because of the medication he was on?"

"What medication?" Deb asked. She went to the bed and lifted Jason's head up by his hair. He grunted. She pried open one eye, then the other.

"We're not sure," Kelly said. "He said last night he wasn't supposed to be drinking because he was on medication. I just wish I knew what he was on."

Tina bent over and rolled Jason on his side, pulling at the waistband of his jeans.

"Ah, Tina . . . ," I began.

"I found this when I was undressing him last night," she explained. There, low on his hip, was a patch.

Deb leaned over and looked. "Oh, my God. Fentanyl. What an idiot." She sat down next to him on the bed and went into another mode completely, the nurse-on-duty mode. She took his pulse and checked his eyes again. Then she reached down his pants and ripped off the patch, throwing it onto the end table.

"This drug is a narcotic. It should never be taken with alcohol. He could have had a very bad reaction to this. It looks like he's just sleeping it off, but he could be out for hours." She shook her head, muttering, "Stupid boy."

We looked at Jason Wilde. His mouth was slightly open, and he was drooling just a little.

Perfect.

"So, now what do we do?" I asked. Okay, I just blew past irritation. Drunken actor in my car—annoying. Unconscious and possible comatose actor in my rented beach house—beyond the pale.

"Do we have to do anything? I mean, he's not doing anybody any harm." Tina looked around at us. "He could just, you know, stay here and sleep it off."

Deb sighed. "Don't you think that someone may start to worry about him? Isn't he filming somewhere? And the girlfriend? Didn't she miss him last night?"

Tina made a face. "I'm pretty sure she wouldn't even notice, Word on the street says they're not all that solid."

"Word on the street?" Deb echoed. She put her hands on her hips and leaned toward Tina. "And what street would that be?"

"Tina, Deb's right," Kelly said. She grabbed the end of a piece of her hair and tugged on it, her only sign of stress. "Somebody needs to know where he is. Listen, we can call the police. Tina, you can get in the car and drive into town, and no one will ever have to know you were even here."

Tina's lip got pouty. "Do we have to?"

"Be reasonable, Tina," I said. "At some point, someone is going to wonder where he is."

At that moment, there was a noise. A buzz. We turned and stared at the end table. It was Jason's phone, obviously on vibrate, and it was thrumming against the tabletop.

"Should we answer it?" Tina asked in a hushed voice.

I grabbed the phone and swiped. "Hello, this is Jason's Wilde's phone."

There was a moment of silence. "Where the hell is Jason? I've been calling him all friggin' night," a rough voice asked.

"The phone was on vibrate. Right now, he's passed out in my guest room," I said.

There was another silence. "Is he naked?"

What a question. "No. We kept his pants on. Who is this?"

"This is his manager, Arthur Sherman. Artie. Who is *this*?"

"Ann Reynolds. Listen, Jason mixed booze and his meds, and he could be out for a while. Can you send somebody over to get him?" I felt so relieved. Jason may have been charming and friendly last night, but it was time we all just moved on.

Artie made a few humming sounds. "Passed out? Is he safe?"

"Sure. I told you, he's in our guest room."

"Our?"

I went into the living room and sat down. Behind me, I could hear the sounds of coffee being made. Crisis averted.

I explained what had happened to Artie, who asked lots of questions about who we were and why we were on Dune Road in the first place. When he was convinced we hadn't taken Jason by force and that he was, in fact, quite safe, he became relaxed and almost friendly.

"Listen, Annie, can I call you Annie? It's a good thing you're doing. Really. Can I ask a favor?"

Deb set down a mug of coffee on the table in front of me. I stared at it longingly. "Sure, Artie."

"Can you just let him stay there until he wakes up?"

"Why?"

"Because if I involve the police or send an ambulance over there to get him, the press might get hold of it. You know and I know what happened, but things like this, well, they can get blown out of proportion."

"Artie, we're on vacation. We have restaurants to eat in, shops to visit, and vineyards to drink our way through. Not to mention a beach right outside our door. We are here to relax and have a good time. No one wants to sit here and babysit Jason until he wakes up."

Tina jumped in front of me. "I do," she squealed. "I want to sit here and babysit Jason."

Artie must have heard her. "See? And to sweeten the pot, I'll give you all a tour of the set on Friday. They're filming in Mattituck."

"Hold on." I held the phone against the couch. "Artie says he'll let us on set on Friday if we let Jason stay here until he wakes up. What do you think?"

Kelly brightened. "That might be fun."

Tina was jumping up and down, tugging on Deb's sleeve. Deb lifted her shoulders, then let them drop.

"Sure. Why not?" Deb said.

I brought the phone back to my ear. "Okay, Artie."

"Good. I'll clear it with the producers and let everyone know where he is. That girlfriend of his is probably going crazy. Just make sure he calls me the minute he wakes up, okay?"

"I will. Bye." I swiped the phone off and looked at Tina. "You'd rather sit here and stare at his unconscious body than go out to a few vineyards?"

I swear her eyes got misty. "It would be an honor."

"Okay. But once he's awake, he's out of here."

"Absolutely," Tina said, nodding her head. "Thanks, Annie."

I put Jason's phone on the table and stared at it. "I don't like that guy," I said, reaching for the coffee and taking a tentative sip.

"Annie, he's letting us tour the set of a television show," Kelly said. "What's not to like?"

The coffee was perfect. I upgraded to a small gulp. "He didn't sound worried about Jason at all. He wanted to know more about us than about him."

Deb sat down with her coffee. "He probably just wanted to make sure his precious client was in good hands. Okay, here is our first 'winging it' decision. Where should we go out to breakfast? That place right in town?"

"Oh, the bagel place?" Kelly asked. "Or the Luncheonette?"

My phone made a noise, and I dug it out of the pocket of my jeans. "Andy says we shouldn't go hiking," I said, reading quickly.

"Well, of course not," Deb said. "Look at this miserable weather. It's like Scotland in November out there. Heathcliff wouldn't take Cathy hiking in this crap."

"He wants to have breakfast." I looked around. "At the Luncheonette."

Kelly leaned forward. "That's perfect. You can meet him there, Deb and I can hang out at the bagel place, and afterward, we can all head out."

"Are you sure you guys don't mind?" I asked. "This is *our* week."

Deb rolled her eyes. "Annie, you haven't shown this much interest in anyone or any thing in months. It's a date, for God's sake. No, we don't mind. Besides, you're being flexible, remember?"

I texted him back, muttering. "It's probably not, like, a real date."

Kelly waved her mug in the air. "Of course it is. He asked you, right?"

"As long as he's paying, it's a date," Tina said. "It's a rule."

I frowned. "Really?" Andy texted back right away. "Oh, gosh. He wants to meet me in, like, thirty minutes."

Deb sprang up. "Thank God we all have our own bathrooms." She looked down at Tina. "You're sure you want to just sit here all day?"

Tina nodded. "I'd hate to have him wake up alone." She reached over and took his phone. "I'll be fine. Honest."

I drank the rest of my coffee. "Okay. Let's roll."

Eckart's Luncheonette is the kind of place that looked like it hitchhiked from Mayberry. It was filled with old-fashioned glass display cabinets, scuffed wooden floors, and wobbly tables. Andy and I sat across from each other and never stopped talking. First, we covered the big issues. We had both voted for the same man for president. We both hated the same football team. We discussed what it would be like to be the first colonists on Mars, and agreed that pets would have to be allowed.

At some point we moved on to quieter, smaller things.

"What do you do all day that you have to wear a suit?" I asked him. "I can rule out baby-seal killer. My next guess was a mortician."

"Wrong answer. Let's just say I keep the world safe for democracy," he said.

I nodded. "Oh. So you're a superhero?"

He chuckled. "Close enough. My cape is in the glove compartment of my car."

"Good to know, because my friends think you're a serial killer, and the only reason you wanted to take me hiking was because it would have been easier to hide my body."

He threw back his head and laughed. "That is very funny. Well, at least you have people looking out for you. And what do you do all day when you're not commingling with the rich and famous out here in the Hamptons?"

"I run the kids' department at my local library. I spend my day reshelving books and keeping children from climbing the walls. Literally. In my spare time, I read every children's book I can get my hands on. I wanted to live with the Swiss Family Robinson, in their tree," I said.

"Me too! Although I must admit, I was a little disappointed when that girl in the kayak showed up."

"And I wanted to *be* the girl in the kayak!"

He smiled. "Maybe we can find our own desert island."

Our knees were touching under the table. I looked down at our hands, which happened to be intertwined. His skin was warm and smooth, and I'd been fixated on a spot right above his left thumb that I was positive would taste just like honey. And there was also something about his lower lip, right in the corner. And I was pretty sure that, underneath his white shirt and very conservative blue-striped tie, his chest would be broad and muscular. I was past the age where six-pack abs were on my must-have list, but I was confident that, shirtless, Andy would not disappoint.

I'd like to point out that I never saw myself as a sex-starved divorcée, ready to jump the bones of any attractive, available man. In fact, as much as I liked having sex with my husband, after we split up there had been no one who even caused a ripple of interest in the libido department. Until Andy. I couldn't decide if it was just my body giving in to pure biology, or something more. Whatever it was, it felt great.

"I know this is your week with your friends," he said. "And I know that's important to you. But can I see you again?"

"Of course," I said. I spoke without thinking. I didn't usually do that. In fact, I never did anything without not only thinking, but overthinking, analyzing, formulating the perfect plan, then thinking about it again. I felt myself starting to grin. "Listen, the best thing about old friends is that they are forgiving. And this year, we all agreed to be more, um, flexible."

"So, tonight?"

I shook my head. "I'm not sure. How about tomorrow? Lunch? Right here in town at Brunetti's?"

He looked heavenward. "She likes Brunetti's. Thank you, God."

I laughed. "I need to go."

He nodded and we left Eckart's. The sun was making a feeble attempt to battle the clouds, and appeared to be losing. Then he put his arms around me and kissed me; it was like an explosion of light and heat and perhaps a celestial choir.

Wow—this guy could really kiss.

I mean, *really* kiss. With lots of tongue. And synchronized hand action. When I finally stepped away, I was thinking that maybe the fog was thick enough that we could have a quickie behind the hydrangea, because no one would be able to see us from the road.

"Are you thinking what I'm thinking?" I finally asked.

"God, I hope so," he answered, his breath ragged.

We spoke at the same time.

"We need to slow down," he said.

"We need a room," I said.

We looked at each other and started to laugh.

"Look at us," he said. "In the middle of town in the middle of the morning."

I could not stop smiling. "Have we scandalized the locals?"

He shook his head and laughed. "The locals probably wouldn't blink." He reached out with his hand and touched my cheek. "I'll see you tomorrow."

He walked away and got into a black, totally nondescript sedan. He waved a hand as he went past. I kind of floated across the street and down the sidewalk, through the door of Goldberg's.

"My God," Kelly said. "Look at that face."

Deb smirked. "I think our girl is in love."

I slid into a seat beside Kelly and put my head on her shoulder. "He's so sweet."

Deb snorted. "Oh, I'm sure."

I sighed. "And he's a really good kisser."

Kelly shrugged me off her shoulder. "Yes, well, after all, that is the important thing."

"Do we know what he does for a living?" Deb asked.

"He's a superhero. He has a cape," I told her.

"Of course he is." Deb glanced at her watch. "Milland's is open. It's Kelly's turn for a little action. Let's get some wine."

Milland Vineyard was in what is called the North Fork on Long Island. We had certain places we revisited every year, and Milland was one of them. They had a blackberry cordial that, when sipped cold and between bites of chocolate, was the equivalent of great sex, but for your taste buds. And, there's Liam.

Ah, Liam. Five years ago, when we first decided to drink our way through the vineyards on Long Island, he had been in charge of one of the tastings at the Milland Vineyard. He was a handsome, charming, but slightly sleazy Irishman, just interesting enough that, when we got back to the house, we spent the night imagining his life story. The favorite fictional scenario was that he was in the Witness Protection Program. The close second was that he was a hit man on the lam from the Boston mob, living his life out as a simple winemaker, always waiting for his crime boss to come through the front door.

Liam always flirted outrageously with Kelly, and she flirted right back, only to feel guilty about it for the entire next day. This year, Kelly was a free agent, and I was interested to see if their battle of wits would take on a different tone.

The main building at Milland Vineyard used to be a barn, and the owners did very little to change it. There was still a cement floor, and large stalls lined the outside walls. There were wine bottles everywhere, of course, but also glasses and cocktail napkins and cheese and post-cards—you could wander in and out of those stalls for an hour or two without seeing everything.

We always walked in and wandered around for a while before we asked for a tasting. And since we got there so early in the season, we were usually the only ones around the big farmhouse table tucked into the corner. Liam had been known, in the past, to open bottles not nec-essarily on the regular tasting menu.

This time Liam followed the sound of our voices and popped his head into an alcove where we were arguing about which Gouda to bring back to the house.

"My favorite ladies from the Garden State," he said, grinning. He was good-looking in a sexy, bad-boy kind of way, even with red hair, blue eyes, and freckles. He had the coloring of a Catholic schoolboy and the body of a professional wrestler, a very interesting combination.

He gave a hug to each of us, saving Kelly for last. For her, there was a kiss on the cheek and a special smile.

"Ah, Kelly, here to break my heart again?" he asked as we walked across the cement floor.

She tossed her blonde hair. "Maybe not, Liam. I'm divorced now. You may have to make good on all those promises you've made over the years."

He stopped dead in his tracks. The smile vanished. He turned and looked at her. "Seriously? You're not married anymore?"

Kelly took a tiny step back. This was obviously not the reaction she'd expected. "Seriously."

Liam glanced at the ground and took a deep breath. "Well." He looked back at her. "I happen to be off tomorrow. I know that you're out here with your friends, and I'd never want to interfere with your plans, but if I give you my number, would you maybe give me a call? Say, for a drink?"

She recovered fast, whipped out her phone, and punched a few buttons. She handed it to him. "Sure. Put it in there. I'll even bump you up to speed dial."

He grabbed the phone, grinning.

The wines for the tasting were amazing.

We had a late lunch at Rowdy Hall. No one famous was there, but we'd grown used to that. Besides, we already had our own personal celebrity, sleeping soundly in our beach house.

We walked around East Hampton until dark. East Hampton was like the adult version of Disney World—clean and well designed, with pretty flowers, chirping birds, and lots of beautiful, smiling people. And there was something for everyone, as long as you had enough money. We strolled, pointed, and sighed a lot more than we actually purchased. Even on sale, a $300 scarf was not really a deal for somebody like me, who thought T. J. Maxx was the place to find a real bargain.

We got home fairly late, and we were all tired. Tina was asleep on the couch with the television on. We tiptoed around her for a few minutes, putting our leftovers in the fridge and dropping our jackets over chairs. Deb opened a beer, found the television remote control, and then settled into the unoccupied corner of the couch while Kelly and I went upstairs to change. We didn't get far.

"Holy crap!" Deb yelled.

Kelly and I were back down in a shot. Deb was standing, staring at the television. Tina was sitting up, squinting and looking confused.

"What? Deb, what's wrong?" I asked.

She pointed at the television.

There were two very attractive news anchors on-screen, and behind them was a picture of Jason Wilde. The woman was speaking.

". . . and although it is too early to consider Wilde a missing person, the production company is very concerned by his absence and has asked local authorities for help."

"What absence are they talking about?" I asked. "He's not a missing person; he's right here." I glared down at Tina. "He *is* right here, isn't he?"

She stood up and shot into her bedroom. We followed.

Yes, there he was, in exactly the same position we'd left him in hours ago.

Deb turned and stomped back into the living room.

We listened to the broadcast, and it was quite a story.

Jason had not reported for his morning call, causing delays on the set of his cable TV show, and also causing a great deal of concern among his coworkers. His girlfriend said he hadn't returned home the night before, but it wasn't the first time, and she didn't start to worry until she hadn't heard from him later in the day. She didn't elaborate as to why or how often he did not return home at night, and the reporter didn't think to ask.

His manager, Arthur Sherman, was especially worried because the actor had been receiving threatening phone calls. The broadcast ended with a local number to call if anyone had information as to his whereabouts.

"Okay, let's call," Deb said.

"Wait," Tina yelped. "You can't. Not while I'm here."

Deb was jabbing her phone with her finger. Very hard. "Then leave."

Tina reached over and snatched the phone away. "Stop, Deb. He should be awake any minute now, right?"

Deb was scowling. "In theory."

"Exactly," Tina said. "So, we'll wait until he wakes up and take him wherever, and, ta-da, we'll have saved the day."

Deb shrugged. "Whatever. But I need something stronger than beer."

We bundled up again, then went out on the deck. Deb had the tequila and Kelly sliced limes. We did a shot, then another, and Tina and Kelly smoked cigarettes in silence. Then, out of the darkness, we heard a familiar yapping.

"What's that scrawny rat doing outside?" Deb groused. "Tina, didn't you shut Muffy up with Jason?"

Tina squinted to the far end of the deck, where the sliders from her room opened up. "Maybe she—oh, God."

We all looked. There was a slender figure standing at the end of the deck. A small, furry object that could only have been Muffy was dancing around. The figure stretched his arms, then brought them down to his sides. A few seconds later, a thin, golden stream could be seen in the faint light coming from the bedroom.

It was Jason Wilde.

He was finally awake.

And pissing off the edge of the deck.

"Thank you, Jesus," Deb said at last.

Chapter Six

We raced into the house, then burst into the bedroom like a horde of crazed groupies. Jason stood by the sliding glass doors, looking scruffy and clueless, zipping up his fly.

He had an amazing body—broad shoulders, six-pack abs. All we'd seen of him for the past twenty-four hours had been his back—which was a very nice back—but his front was memorable.

"Ah . . ." He closed his eyes and shook his head.

Deb moved forward slowly. "Hey, Jason, you've been asleep for a while. I'm a nurse. Can I just check you out? See if you're okay?"

He nodded and stumbled against the bed, then sat down at the end of the mattress.

Deb knelt beside him, checked his pulse, and looked into both of his eyes.

"Do you know who you are?"

"Jason."

"Very good. What month is this?"

"May."

"Good. Do you know where you are?"

He looked around. "No clue."

Deb smiled. "Where's the last place you remember being?"

He frowned. "The American."

"Yes. You were at the American, and you drank, and you had a very bad reaction to your medication. You've been asleep for an entire day."

It took him a moment to digest that fact, and then he buried his head in his hands. "Shit. I missed my call this morning."

Deb nodded. "Yes, you did."

"Ah, Jason?" I edged around so he could see me. "Your agent called you this morning. Artie?"

Jason squinted. "Artie Sherman? He's my manager."

"Right. Yes, he said that. Anyway, he also said he'd speak to the producers and tell everyone you were all right. But something happened. He didn't, and people are worried about you, including the police. You need to call him right away."

He looked around groggily. "Where's my phone?" he asked. Muffy jumped up on the bed to settle onto Jason's lap, tail wagging furiously. He actually smiled and scratched her head.

Kelly took his phone off the end table and handed it to him. "Here, Jason."

He stared at her. "I remember you," he said slowly.

Tina pushed her way forward. "Do you remember me, too, Jason? Tina? We were supposed to have a date. Tonight!"

He scowled and cradled his phone. "Can I have some privacy?"

We all backed out of the bedroom and sat quietly around the fireplace.

"It was kind of exciting, having him here," Kelly said. "Even if he was asleep the whole time."

Deb nodded. "True. How often do you get to spend the night under the same roof as a television star? Especially a missing television star."

Tina cleared her throat. "Well, we could invite him to stay another night. I mean, he's all sleepy and stuff. And it's kind of late." She looked around hopefully. "What do you think?"

Deb shook her head. "Tina, get real. He's got a girlfriend; he missed a day's shooting, and he probably has five hundred things to square away. Including the police. Sorry, but I think our little adventure is coming to an end."

Tina's shoulders slumped. I felt kind of sad for her. I'm sure the night she spent with Jason was not what she had envisioned.

"Just think, Tina," I said. "You not only had a drink with him, you got to carry him up a flight of stairs, take his clothes off, and sleep in the bed right next to his. Not too shabby."

Jason came out of the bedroom looking rumpled but sexy. "Ah, hey, everyone, can I just crash here again tonight?"

Deb's head snapped around. "What?"

He shrugged. "Artie said I should just rest up and not worry about anything. He said that he's got a plan worked out, and I should just sit tight. Do you all mind?" He was grinning sheepishly, looking all sweet and adorable.

"Why didn't Artie tell people where you were?" I asked. Something felt wrong here. "Why did he let this go on for so long?"

Jason rubbed his face with both hands. "Artie said it sparked a lot of interest, you know, the news and stuff. It's good for the show. It's good for me."

"Oh?" My BS meter went into overdrive. "Why did he let the local authorities, which, by the way, means police, get involved?" I glanced at Kelly. She was concentrating on his body. Deb, however, was still not happy.

"Annie has a point. Having the police involved brings things to another level," she said.

Jason tilted his head at her. "We haven't met." He smiled. The air suddenly vibrated with boyish charm. How did he do that? He crossed over and held out his hand. "Jason. Thanks for taking such good care of me."

Deb turned into a marshmallow, a smiling, almost-giggling marshmallow, as she took his hand. "Deborah. Deb. Well, it's what I do."

He leaned close to her. "And you're really good at it."

He had managed to say the magic words. Deb had always been the hard-working, totally unappreciated person in our group, who organized carpools and fund-raisers for Little League, ran bake sales, and hauled donations to our local women's shelter. She spent a great deal of time driving her sports-crazed kids all over the state, all the while working grueling shifts as a nurse. She was crazy about her kids, adored her husband of thirty years, and was a great friend. But because she was not normally warm and fluffy, people tended to not give her all the pats on the back she deserved. And here was Jason Wilde—handsome, charming, and built for sin—praising her for a job well done.

Score two points for Jason.

He straightened. "I hate to impose on you kind ladies any longer, really I do, but like I said, Artie has a plan. He'll get in touch with me in the morning, and we can go from there. What do you think?"

He had not answered my question. Allowing the police into this made me nervous. I thought there was something rotten in Denmark, but I could see I was outvoted. Kelly smiled dreamily.

"Well, I guess it would be okay," Deb said, in a tone that suggested she maybe hadn't drunk all the Kool-Aid, but she had taken at least a sip.

Tina was practically levitating with excitement. "Of course you can stay. We'd love it," she squeaked. She bounded over. "Can I get you anything? Food? Something to drink?"

He looked at her through half-closed eyes. "Ah, sure. But first, can I, like, shower?"

She nodded. "Follow me."

They disappeared around the corner.

Deb raised an eyebrow. "Do you think she'll offer to scrub his back?"

Kelly stretched out on the couch and reached for the remote. "Five bucks says we won't see them until the morning."

Deb snorted. "I won't bet against that. Annie, any more tequila?"

"Listen, guys, if Tina does, well, whatever, I don't really want to be this close. You know?" I looked at Kelly, who rolled her eyes.

"God, you're right," she said. "Let's move the party upstairs."

We took the bottle and some lemons and salt and crowded into my room, where we watched the Food Network until we were happily drunk and sleepy. I turned off the television, only to hear Muffy whimpering and making noises like scratches against a closed door. So I turned the television back on and fell asleep.

I had a vague feeling of sunlight on my face. I squinted. Yes, it was there. Sun. Streaming through the open door. At last. And I remembered that I was having lunch with Andy. I sighed with contentment. What an amazing morning.

"Annie? Wake up. Now."

It was Kelly. I sat up. Deb was snoring next to me in the large bed.

"What's up?"

She ran over and hopped into the bed. "You won't believe what's going on." She found the remote, turned up the volume, and clicked to the local station. The same two people we had seen last night were back, but the story had changed.

". . . has confirmed that a ransom note was received. The FBI has been notified, and three middle-aged women are being sought in connection with the crime."

Kelly looked at me. "A note? Someone sent a ransom note?"

Deb rolled over and sat up, and we all stared at the screen. Across the bottom, words ran in a continuous loop: POLICE CONFIRM RANSOM NOTE RECEIVED IN DISAPPEARANCE OF ACTOR JASON WILDE.

According to the anchorwoman, a ransom note had been slipped under the door of Jason's rented home and was found by his girlfriend at a little after eight in the morning. The security cameras had not been turned on, it was explained, and no one was seen near the house at the time. The police had not been at the house when the note was found, although they had now established a presence in case of any further communication. The FBI, of course, was now handling the situation.

"What the . . . ," Deb muttered.

"They're looking for us," I whispered, trying to keep the quiver in my voice down to a minimum. I had never so much as gotten a speeding ticket in my whole life, and now I was wanted for questioning. For a kidnapping. Something was spreading through my chest—panic, fear, whatever—and I could barely breathe. "Three middle-aged women. That's us. You get thrown in prison for kidnapping." I think my brain exploded for a moment while I imagined myself in an orange jumpsuit, begging my daughter through a thick glass window to bring more cigarettes and chocolate bars.

"Not me," Deb said. "You're the kidnappers. I'm just your innocent black friend."

"Nobody's going to prison, because we're not kidnappers," Kelly said. "We just gave him a ride."

"But the police don't know that," I said. I was feeling more than just a little panicked. I was also starting to feel angry. What had happened to put us in this position? Somewhere out there was someone to blame, and I wanted to know who it was. "Who would have sent a ransom note?"

"Wait," Kelly said. "Oh, no. Look."

Julio, the bartender at the American Hotel on Monday night, was being interviewed. "They came in late, after nine," he said. "Nice ladies. Sat in the lobby. The one with the spiky purple hair asked if Jason had been in, and I said no, but he usually didn't show until later. They had a drink, and in walked Jason. The purple-haired one called him over right away, invited him to sit with them. The blonde asked for another round. Then Jason bought a round of shots, put it on his tab. They all talked. Jason seemed drunk, and after a few minutes, they all left together."

A stunning Asian woman holding a microphone conducted the interview. "What about the third woman?" she asked.

Julio shrugged. "She didn't drink. Had a ginger ale. Didn't say much to Jason. I think she was the driver."

The interviewer turned to the camera. "The women are believed to be driving a late-model silver minivan with New Jersey plates. Back to you, Mike."

"Purple hair," I muttered, feeling suddenly grateful that at least I now had a target for my anger. "Where is Tina?"

Deb threw off the covers. "Forget Tina. Where is that boy? He needs to call that manager of his right now."

We went downstairs. Tina's bedroom door was standing open, the room empty except for Muffy curled comfortably on a very wrinkled bed. The dog growled softly at us. We could hear the shower running.

"Are they in there together?" Kelly asked, looking toward the bathroom door.

I looked around the room. "Where are Tina's suitcases? And her shoes?"

Kelly whirled around and ran into the living room, calling for Tina. I ran to the front door and opened it just in time to see a large yellow cab inch its way back down the long driveway to the street.

"Hey," I yelled. I ran down the stairs in my bare feet. It was really cold. The sand felt rough between my toes, and I turned just in time to see the cab back down the drive.

I screamed her name. I ran after the cab, even as it turned onto Dune Road. I stomped my feet and had a perfect little tantrum right there in the middle of the street.

Tina left? Just like that? Without a word? I was filled with pure unadulterated rage at her complete lack of consideration, though a small part of me was also wondering if sex with Jason Wilde often yielded that kind of result.

I went back up into the house. The television was on, Jason's picture still splashed across the screen. Deb was making coffee, looking furious. Kelly had a melon in one hand and a very long knife in the other.

"Is she gone?" she asked, waving the blade around.

I nodded. "Yes. At least she left us the tequila."

"And Muffy," Deb said. "Let's not forget Muffy."

"But . . . why?" Kelly asked. "I mean, he slept with her. Which was exactly what she wanted. Was he really that bad?"

The shower went off. We sat at the table and waited for Jason. He came in, Muffy scampering at his heels, towel wrapped around his waist, water glistening off all his muscled parts.

"Morning," he said cheerfully. "Who's making breakfast?"

I leaned forward, controlling the urge to leap across the table and grab his blond hair with both hands. "Jason, you're on the news again this morning. You've been upgraded from a missing person to a kidnapping victim. What the hell is going on here? I thought good old Artie took care of everything."

Jason looked down, then to the side, and finally out the window. "Can I get some coffee?"

"You can get it yourself," Deb snarled. "Do you have any idea what's going on?"

He shrugged. "Well, Artie saw what was happening after the story broke about me being missing, and thought he'd take advantage. So he sent a ransom note early this morning."

"What!" Deb brought both her hands, well, fists, down on the table, causing cutlery, keys, pretty much everything to jump. "He sent the note himself?"

Jason held out both hands, palms up. "Listen, ladies, I know this sounds like, but it's no big deal. Believe me. Artie explained it all to me." He looked around. "Wait, where's Tina?"

Kelly stabbed the melon with her knife. "She left."

His eyes widened. "Tina left? When?"

"While you were in the shower, lover boy," Deb snapped. "What happened?"

He pulled out a chair and sat. "Listen, can I tell you something about Tina? Very weird chick, okay? She kept wanting to, like, reen-act scenes from the TV show. Sex stuff, you know?" He ran his hand through his wet hair. "It kind of freaked me out."

I closed my eyes briefly. I really did not want to hear this. "Jason, let's get back to being kidnapped. What exactly is supposed to happen here?" I asked.

"Yeah, well, about that." He was looking out the windows again. "I'm just going to sit tight here for the rest of the week. The press is all over this. I'm trending on Twitter. This could be a giant break for me. I mean, look, I've made national news."

He got up and stood in front of the TV screen. The sun was stream-ing through the windows, and his body practically glowed. He reached for the remote and turned up the volume. "Check it out. Don't I look great up there?"

"How can you do this?" Deb asked, hands on hips. "What about your family? Your girlfriend? How can you let people worry about you?"

He shrugged. "Hey, I trust Artie. He told me to stay put. He said he'd take care of everything."

"But Jason, the FBI is involved. I mean, this is going to get really serious very quickly. And we are wanted for questioning." When I was thinking about a little adventure in my life, this was not what I'd imagined. Meeting a tall, dark, handsome stranger? That was exciting. Being wanted for a crime—not so much. "You have to go to the police and tell them it was a big mistake."

He kept his eyes fixed on the television. "No, Annie. I can't do that. Sorry."

I glanced over at Kelly. Her jaw was set. Worse, she was tugging on her hair. "And what if we go to the police?" she asked.

He turned to look at us then. He looked apologetic but determined. "You won't. It's my word against yours. I would say I was drugged and you brought me here against my will. You kept me here for a whole day without notifying the police. That could be considered unlawful restraint at best, or at worst, kidnapping." He spoke very courteously, and he was obviously parroting someone else's words.

"What?" Kelly asked.

"Unlawful restraint. You know, restraining a person," Jason explained, frowning. "Unlawfully. It's a thing." He straightened his shoulders. "Or I could go with kidnapping. Either way, I could have you all thrown in jail."

Deb was practically snarling. "Did Artie tell you all that? Because that does not sound like something you would just know all about."

Jason crossed over to the kitchen, opened a few cabinets until he found the coffee mugs, poured himself a cup, then leaned back, looking at us coolly, but still managing to stay an arm's length away from Kelly and her knife. "I think it's more Leo's idea. Artie's brother. Leo's the real brains, you know? Artie is more on the artistic side."

"Those threats Artie said you got," Deb said. "The phone calls. Were they real?"

Jason shrugged. "Threats? Nah, people like me. Artie made all that up. To add more drama, you know?" He took a long drink of coffee. "It will be no big deal. You do whatever you were going to do, and I'll hang here, watch some television, catch up on my sleep, whatever. How bad can it be? And in return, you'll get the VIP treatment when you visit the set." He grinned again, but the effect had vanished.

"We don't want you here," I said.

"Ah, don't say that. I'm a cool guy. I won't be in the way. Honest. A little food, a little beer, and I'm good." He looked around. "Do any of you have an iPhone charger? My phone died."

"Jason," I said slowly. My feelings toward him, which had not exactly been warm and fuzzy in the first place, had taken a definite turn. "Who would you call? You're supposed to be tied to the radiator in some abandoned building, surrounded by a group of vicious kidnappers, remember?"

He grinned and shrugged. Ten minutes ago he would have been adorable. "Yeah, I know. But I want to, you know, check Twitter, see what people are saying. Besides, Artie might call again."

"The last thing you need," Deb snapped, "is more advice from that blithering idiot. Besides, if you want to know what's going on, you can watch the news."

"But," he said, his voice getting a bit whiny, "I should be checking my fan page. I can't do that without my phone."

Kelly walked over to him and put her hand on his shoulder. "This is not your television show, Jason. This is the real world. And in the real world, when you're being held hostage by three evil and desperate women, you have to learn to do without."

"Ah, come on," he said. "Don't be like that. You aren't desperate, are you? I know you're not evil. You all took care of me. You are the kind of women who adopt puppies and kiss bruised knees. Pretend I'm a lost kitten. This could be fun."

"No," I said. "It can't be fun. At all. At least, not for us. And you are not a lost kitten; you're an unwanted guest. So trust me when I tell you that we're going to make sure it's not fun for you either."

He shrugged. "Whatever. I'm going to get dressed and finish my coffee," he said. "Then I'll have something for breakfast. Eggs, I think. I like them sunny-side up. And then I think I'm going right back to sleep. Funny, huh? Asleep for a whole day and I'm still tired. See you gals in a bit." He rose and walked back toward his room. Halfway there, the towel around his hips loosened and slipped off. He didn't even slow down.

His butt was amazing.

"Now what?" Kelly whispered.

Deb shook her head slowly. "We could take pictures of that ass and sell them on the Internet." She made a rude noise. "That boy obviously never had his ass whipped as a child. Rudest young man ever. Well, if he thinks he can ruin our time together, he's wrong. We'll just leave him here, go off for the day, and I bet he'll change his mind quick enough. Without somebody waiting on him and catering to his every whim, he'll get bored and beg this Artie person to come rescue him."

I breathed a sigh of relief. Of course. He was used to adoring fans and paid minions. I'd watched *Entourage*. I knew what kind of treatment he expected. I had to admit, he almost had me at "kiss bruised knees," but I was made of stronger stuff. "That makes sense. He's probably not used to doing things for himself. I bet he doesn't last the day."

"Okay, then. Let's go," Deb said, heading for her room.

"Now?" Kelly said. "Where?"

"Anywhere," Deb said. "I'm not going to hang around here and wait on this clown."

"Do you really think there is a thing called unlawful restraint?" Kelly asked.

I shrugged. "No idea. Isn't there a legal Q&A site on the Internet somewhere? Maybe we could ask."

"Maybe," Deb said. "But not right now."

I hadn't showered, but I didn't care. I raced upstairs for shoes and my purse, Kelly right behind me. When we came downstairs a few minutes later, we could hear the blow-dryer going. Deb drew the drapes across the windows at the back of the house, blocking the view, both inside and out. The last thing we needed was somebody coming up the public path from the beach to get a look at Jason lounging in our living room. We closed the front door quietly behind us and hurried down the outside steps. I was starting to back the car out when Deb let out a very loud, nasty word.

"We can't drive anywhere," she said.

I put on the brakes. "Why not?"

"They're looking for three women in a silver minivan with Jersey plates, remember?"

We were lucky; 461 Dune Road stood two houses in from the road. The drive passed other homes before ending at our parking spot, so there was no way any car, not even my smoking-hot silver van, could be seen from the road.

But on the road . . .

I turned off the ignition. I suddenly wanted to cry. I wanted to throw back my head and howl. Instead, I pounded the steering wheel. "We need to be able to get out of here."

Kelly was leaning back in the seat next to me, eyes closed. "Why? We don't have to go anywhere. We can just spend the rest of the week sitting on the deck and looking at the ocean, getting drunk."

"No, we can't," I said. "Even when Jason decides to stop being kidnapped, do you think the FBI will just give up and forget the whole thing? We're wanted for questioning. We will *always* be wanted for questioning. We probably won't be able to drive off the island to go home."

Deb swore again. "You're right, Annie. We need to fix this."

"How?" Kelly asked.

I was thinking hard. "We need to find Artie Sherman and have him get Jason out of here. Then we need a story that will send the police and everybody looking in a different direction so we can get the hell out of Dodge."

"And how are we supposed to find Artie?" Deb asked.

I was staring ahead. "I bet the people who work on the show would know how to find him. We just need to find out where they're shooting, get somebody talking, then track down Artie and convince him what a bad idea this is. Then we can go back to being on vacation."

"Oh, really? Is that all we have to do?" Deb's voice had a slightly sarcastic edge. "That should be easy."

My cell phone made a noise. I dug it out of my purse. A text from Andy.

"Andy just cancelled lunch. He says something happened at work. Just as well." I texted him back. I hadn't realized how much I'd been looking forward to seeing him until I had to tell him, "No prob."

Kelly's mouth was in a thin, hard line. "We can rent a car," she said. She was on her phone. "I bet there are lots of car-rental places."

"And I bet they're all being watched in case a woman from New Jersey needs to make a quick getaway," Deb said.

Kelly dropped the phone on her lap. We were quiet for a few minutes.

"Maybe we can get someone to rent a car for us," I said.

Deb said, "I can rent the car; nobody's looking for a little old black lady. They're all looking for you two and Tina of the purple hair."

"But we need a ride there," Kelly said. "Although I guess we could walk. It's only six miles."

Deb raised an eyebrow. "I'm not walking six miles for anything. Can we call a cab?"

"Won't they be watching cab companies too? The FBI, I mean," I said.

"Probably," Deb said. "We need a ride. I wish we knew somebody out here."

I turned to Kelly. "Call Liam."

Her eyes opened wide. "Liam?"

"He can take us to the car-rental place. He said he wasn't working today. He'd probably race over here to help you out."

She shook her head. "I don't want to take advantage."

"Why not?" asked Deb. "If you feel guilty, offer him a quickie."

I snorted and looked back at Kelly. Her phone was in her hand.

"What should I ask him?" she said.

"Have him meet you at John Scott's for breakfast," Deb suggested.

She shook her head. "They're not open for breakfast."

My heart sank a bit lower. I was starving.

"Then just ask him to pick you up here," I said. "We'll think of something."

Kelly hit a button and held the phone to her ear. "Liam? It's Kelly. I need a favor."

She listened, and I swear she blushed. "Well, how about you come out to the house and take me to breakfast." He must have agreed, because she went into a long, detailed explanation of where to turn and how the drive went past two empty houses. She was beginning to describe the walkway to the beach when Deb reached over and smacked her hand. Kelly said good-bye and sat back, sighing.

"I feel terrible," she moaned.

"Why?" Deb asked. "He likes you. You, I'm fairly certain, like him, and now you're having breakfast together. Aside from the fact that he's also aiding and abetting, you have nothing to feel bad about."

I stared out the window. The sun was shining. It was warm. "Let's wait on the beach," I said. "He won't be here for a while."

Kelly nodded. "He said about twenty minutes."

We got out and then walked to the ocean. It was beautiful. The sky was finally clear, and there was no wind. We sat in the sand, and I tried not to think about life in a federal prison.

"So we'll just ask him to drive us, right?" Kelly finally asked.

"Right," Deb said.

"And what, exactly, do I tell Liam about why we can't do that for ourselves?"

I was stuck. I glanced at Deb. She looked equally clueless.

"Guys," Kelly urged, "come on. We need a reasonable excuse for him to do this."

"Tell him that the minivan is broken down," I said, warming up to the idea. "And the garage can't get it until tomorrow. Just ask him to take us to the car-rental place. He can drop off Deb and me, take you to breakfast, and no harm, no foul. Once we have wheels, we can find Artie."

"I still don't know how we're going to do that," Deb said.

"We'll figure it out," I said. "Trust me."

Kelly sighed. "I do. You always come up with something. Liam should be here in few minutes. Let's head back. If he knocks on the door, Jason will probably answer it."

We were sitting on the steps when Liam pulled up in a battered Mercedes. He got out and looked at us cautiously.

"What's up?" he asked.

Kelly got to him first and slipped her arm through his. "The van crapped out. Could you drop Deb and Annie at the car rental in town? Then you and I can have breakfast somewhere."

He nodded and then glanced over at my car. His face didn't change, but I had the feeling that the silver minivan with Jersey plates registered somewhere.

We all got into his car. When we reached the rental place, he dropped off Deb and me and drove away with Kelly. Deb had no problem getting us a nice Prius. The two of us had breakfast, then texted Kelly to let her know we were ready to start Operation Find Artie Sherman. Deb and I waited almost half an hour for Liam to drop her off back in Westhampton Beach. She was a little flushed and looked quite happy when she walked up to us.

"Okay, let's go," she said.

"Nice breakfast?" Deb asked as she pulled away from the curb.

Kelly took out her phone, and her fingers started flying. She was grinning. "Yes. A great breakfast, actually. Liam has been out to see Jason's show being filmed a couple of times. Security is very tight, he said. He also said they probably aren't shooting if their star is MIA. However, he did give me a few names . . . wait, here she is. The Facebook page for the makeup artist on set says that she's heading to Bridgehampton for a day of shopping. She's looking for wineglasses. That means there's no work on the set today."

"He knows the makeup person?" Deb asked.

"He knows everybody," Kelly said. "At least ten people said hello to him in the restaurant, and three more people waved as we were crossing the street."

"So, what do we do?" I asked. "Find this makeup person and strike up a conversation with her, and hope she knows something about Artie?"

"Liam says the makeup and hair people know all the gossip," Kelly said.

"Do we even know what she looks like?" Deb asked.

"Yes. Her picture is on her Facebook page," Kelly said. "But she'll probably be done with her shopping by the time we get there."

"No problem," Deb said. "She's a woman. We know how women think. After shopping, she's either getting wine or ice cream. We split up, stake out a few places, and find her."

"And then what?" I asked.

Kelly had been fixated on her phone. "She's a dog lover."

"Damn," Deb muttered. "I knew we should have brought Muffy along."

"Seriously, guys. She's a dog lover, a vegan, and from Detroit."

"Perfect," I said. "So, whoever finds her first needs to talk puppies, quinoa, and cars. Easy."

"We can do this," Kelly said. "We're all smart and friendly women. Surely we can accidentally bump into her and engage her in conversation. I bet she'd be bursting to talk about Jason. All we have to do is play the innocent tourist. Her name is Maureen McKenna."

We drove into Bridgehampton and found a parking spot right away. Already, it seemed like the gods were on our side. Kelly had been on her phone, getting the shopping scoop. We all looked at Maureen's pictures. We were each assigned two stores. We had our cell phones turned on. I felt nervous and a little scared. What if we actually found this person? I wish I had paid more attention to the plotlines of *Castle*.

It took me about ten minutes to arrive at my first assignment. It was a lovely little boutique tucked along a side street that had really unusual household things, mostly imported from France. No glassware, but I did see some very nice cotton towels that cost as much as my first dishwasher.

I was headed to my second shop when I got a text from Kelly. Maureen had been sighted. She gave the address.

We all converged outside a small coffee shop. Kelly gestured for us to follow her inside. We went in, single file, and stood in the line for coffee. Kelly motioned with her head.

A woman was seated by herself near the window, surrounded by shopping bags. She was sitting down but seemed very tall and painfully thin. She looked only vaguely like the picture on Facebook. Her hair was cut short on one side and shaved on the other. The color was blue.

She had quite a large tattoo on her forearm, and another going down her leg. Her nose appeared to be pierced. So were both of her ears, her eyebrow (twice), and her upper lip.

Kelly whispered, "Pretend we're not together. Annie, you're at the end. We'll take the two empty tables, so you could ask to sit with her. Got it?"

Me? Oh, no. Why me? And since when had Kelly become such a master manipulator? I was the one who did all the planning, *not* the doing.

I drifted away from the line to examine a shelf of coffee-themed merchandise on display, further distancing myself. By the time I finally ordered and received my soy chai latte, all the tables were indeed full.

I gripped my cup with both hands but then put it down. It was *really* hot. I grabbed a couple of napkins and tried again, moving casually to the window.

"Ah, I'm sorry, but could I grab this seat?" I asked.

Maureen looked up from her phone and shrugged. "Sure."

I sat down gingerly. On closer inspection, she looked about fourteen years old, despite the heavy eyeliner, dark lipstick, and rampant accessorizing.

I sipped. Where should I start? Dogs? Tofu? The water crisis in Detroit? I glanced at her. She was fixated on her phone. Was I just supposed to start chatting with her?

I sipped again. Forget subtle. I was too anxious for subtle. I leaned toward her. "Did you hear what happened to Jason Wilde? The actor? Kidnapped, right here in the Hamptons."

Maureen's head snapped up. She glanced around. "I work with him. On the set."

I let my jaw drop. "No!"

She nodded, looking very smug. "Oh, yes. It's devastating. We have no idea what will happen to the show."

"Not to mention Jason."

She shifted conspiratorially in her seat and lowered her voice. "Can I tell you something? Jason Wilde is a terrible actor. Luckily, most of the time he's just himself on camera, and that works fine because he really is charming and likable. If he has to actually act, he's awful. He can't cry, show fear, get angry—he's like a mannequin. But we love him. All of us." Her eyes filled with tears. "I can't bear to think of him being hurt."

I felt so bad for her. I wanted to tell her not to worry, that Jason was safe and comfortable and being guarded by the most devoted of watchdogs.

"I never thought he was a great actor," I said, trying to keep the conversation going. "I guess it's nice to know he's a good person."

Maureen sniffed. "He is on a first-name basis with everyone. He treats us all the same. He's a real people person. I mean, when he talks to you, he sincerely cares, you know?"

"Really? I kind of figured he was one of those self-centered types, you know, who do whatever they want without thinking about the consequences to others."

She leaned forward and glanced around again. "Jason is not, shall we say, the brightest bulb in the box. Thinking about anything is not his specialty. But he loves people. He gets them. He can see into your soul." She leaned back and took a deep breath.

"That's why everyone is so upset," she continued. "Except for the director, of course, but they had been sleeping together and it ended badly. The producer is a wreck. So is his manager, who has his nose so far up Jason's butt it's embarrassing."

Artie. She knew Artie! Perfect. Now, just a little more information . . . "What's everyone doing while the set is shut down?"

She shrugged. "Most of us are shopping. The schedule is brutal. We never get time off because Jason needs, like, a hundred takes of every scene. The man can't act thirsty in the middle of a desert. We don't really mind, you know, but still . . ."

Yeah, yeah. Okay, Maureen, enough with the miserable problems of the people who get to *work on television*. "But I suppose the producer and, um, this Artie person are waiting by the phone. You know, in case the kidnapper calls."

Maureen shrugged again. It appeared to be her main form of expression. "The FBI has swooped in and is handling everything. They're on set, at the house with his girlfriend—hell, they're everywhere. I'm sure Artie is doing what he does most days, sitting in a crap bar in Hampton Bays, drinking like a fish and wondering how long his meal ticket is going to last."

Bingo! I wondered how many crap bars there were in Hampton Bays. I took another sip of my latte. "Well, I hope they find Jason safe and sound so you can get back to work."

Another shrug. "They're in the process of writing him off the show anyway. His contract is up, and rumor has it they're going to shift the focus to the character that is his assistant on the show. The actor's younger and can actually walk and speak at the same time. That's the hardest thing, you know? Even if they find Jason, he won't be on the show much longer. And the guy who plays the assistant? Sure, he may be all *Actors Studio* and shit, but he's a real pain-in-the-ass prima donna."

My mind was spinning so fast I was getting dizzy. "Well, thanks for sharing your table. And all that great gossip. I hope everything works out." I said good-bye and practically ran out onto the sidewalk.

We were not very good at being inconspicuous. Deb and Kelly came out after me in quick succession.

"Weren't you supposed to wait or something?" I groused.

Deb rolled her eyes. "What did Maureen say?"

I told them about the conversation as we began walking back to the car.

"He's being written out of the show? Well, that explains why his manager is so desperate for the publicity," Kelly said.

"And we know where to find him," I said. "Maureen said he drinks in a crap bar in Hampton Bays."

Deb frowned. "There are crap bars here? In the Hamptons?"

"There are crap bars everywhere," I said, climbing into the backseat. "Kelly, get us to Hampton Bays."

According to Yelp, there were nine bars in Hampton Bays. Kelly looked at all of them, and by the time we passed the city-limit sign, she had mapped out a strategy.

"We'll start at this place called Mike's. Everyone still calls it by its old name, Bubba's, and bar fights start there frequently."

"And how, exactly, do we explain ourselves going into a place like that?" Deb asked.

We all thought.

Finally, I said, "Kelly, you have to go in. Ask for Artie. Tell whomever that he was supposed to be helping you get a role on the show. I bet he's just the type of scumbag who'd sleep with a woman on the pretext of trying to help her career."

Kelly shivered. "Sure. But why me?"

"Because," Deb told her, "you're the closest we've got to an aging starlet type. It would be better if you were thirty, but we can't have everything."

"No problem."

We found Mike's. The sign still read **BUBBA'S**. There were six pickup trucks and three motorcycles parked out front, as well as a twenty-year-old Impala and a station wagon dating from the '70s.

"Is this still the Hamptons?" Kelly asked in a hushed voice.

Deb cut the engine. "Not everybody is a millionaire. Some people have to work the real jobs, like pumping gas and hauling building supplies."

"And they all hang out here," I said. "Good luck."

Kelly turned to me. "Come on."

"Me? You want me to go in there? Oh, Kelly, no."

"Yes. I need you. Besides, this was your idea."

She gave me that look, and I got out of the car. We could hear Elvis singing inside.

"Can we do this?" I asked.

"I minored in theater in college," Kelly said. "I was Amanda in *The Glass Menagerie* my junior year." She lifted her blonde head and marched into that dive bar like she owned the place.

Chapter Seven

There were three guys in ball caps and jeans playing pool, and a dozen more men at the bar. There were no women in the place, and as we entered, I can't say for sure, but it seemed that all conversation stopped. Maybe Elvis just started singing louder.

Kelly never faltered. She paused—like a gazelle sniffing the air for the scent of a lion—then went straight to the bartender.

"Artie Sherman was supposed to meet me here. Has he been in yet?"

My God, the woman was masterful. Her voice didn't shake; she seemed poised and confident, and even a bit irritated that Artie wasn't where he said he'd be. She sure made an impression on the bartender, who swallowed hard and looked very apologetic.

"Sorry, miss, but Artie left a little while ago. He didn't say he was waiting for nobody."

Her jaw clenched. She was either an excellent actress or fighting her urge to correct his grammar. She sighed heavily and shook her head.

"The man is a complete bastard. I knew he was lying to me." Was her lower lip really quivering? "He promised!" She looked at me. "You were right."

What? Was I in on this as well? I swallowed hard. "I could smell the skunk on him from across the room," I said, in almost a snarl.

She leaned over the bar. "When does he usually come in?" she asked the bartender, in a you-and-me-against-the-world kind of way.

The bartender glanced around the room. So did I. Every man in the place was watching Kelly. He lowered his voice. "Right before lunch. I won't tell him you were here."

Kelly straightened up and tossed her hair. "I owe you," she said. She adjusted her purse on her shoulder and smoothed the front of her shirt. In that moment, one of the guys at the bar slid closer.

"Maybe you ladies would care for a drink?" he asked.

I sighed to myself. Really? Kelly was going to get hit on? In a dive bar in the Hamptons? The guy was about forty, with dark hair slicked back and a missing tooth. He was wearing jeans, a black T-shirt, and a Boston Red Sox baseball cap.

Kelly smiled and looked grateful. "That would be divine," she purred.

I leaned against the bar and tried to look like a piece of it. I prayed silently that no one would notice me.

The guy looked at the bartender. "Ed, you got any champagne back there?"

Ed froze, a distinctive deer-in-the-headlights look in his eye.

Kelly waved a hand. "White wine will do," she said. She glanced at me. "The same?"

I nodded. Ed looked relieved and found two wineglasses. Even in the dim light, I could see an obvious thumbprint on one glass, and dried splash marks on the other. He poured wine from an unmarked bottle.

Kelly took the glass without wincing and drank bravely. "Thanks. I'm Kelly."

The guy at the bar took a long drink of his Bud Lite. "Larry."

She smiled, lighting up half the bar. "Pleased to meet you, Larry. I appreciate the wine. I don't often drink this time of day, but . . ."

Larry grinned. "So, you're an actress?"

Kelly nodded. I looked around the bar. The pool game had resumed, Elvis had stopped singing, and there was a rumble of background noise. Larry had staked his claim, and the rest of the crowd was respecting his space. I relaxed.

I shouldn't have.

"I'm George," a voice said at my elbow.

I turned, and a rather short, somewhat stocky man, maybe my age, with all his teeth, was smiling at me.

"Are you an actress too?" he asked.

I bit my lip to keep my mouth from dropping open. I turned my head to glare at Kelly.

She laughed, almost gaily, and put her arm around my shoulder. "No, she's just a friend. A *good* friend, if you catch my drift."

My newfound admirer quickly stepped back. Larry paled. I grabbed my smudged wineglass and gulped the contents like a shot.

"Well, we should go," Kelly said. "But we'll be back tomorrow." She winked at Larry, spun around, and walked out. I scurried after her.

Once outside, Kelly sprinted to the car and scrambled into the backseat. I followed, feeling nauseous.

"Kelly, you were amazing!" I said as I slammed the door shut.

She grinned. "Yeah, I was. Deb, go. Quick."

Deb peeled out of the drive. "What happened?" she asked.

"Kelly was unbelievable," I blurted out. "She walked in there like the queen bee, and, well, first she got the bartender to tell us when Artie would be around, then she got us free drinks—that tasted like rubbing alcohol, but still—then she chased away two wannabes by playing the lesbian card. What a show."

Kelly beamed modestly.

Deb glanced back from the front seat. "How about you, Annie?"

The rush of adrenaline that had gotten me in and out of Mike's vanished, leaving me a bit lightheaded. "I think I may faint."

"Should we pull over?" Deb asked.

Kelly pushed my head between my knees. "She'll be fine," she said.

"Okay, then," Deb said. "When can we catch Artie?"

"He's there before lunch," Kelly said. "We'll go back tomorrow and get that sneaky bastard." She looked at me. "See? Fun and excitement."

"Maybe," I said. "If we don't all end up in jail."

When we got home, we were tired, cranky, and starving. All I wanted to do was sit down, open up a few more quarts of chowder, have some wine, and fall asleep in front of the television.

But—

There was a motorcycle parked next to my minivan.

Kelly and I stared in silence, and Deb muttered something positively objectionable.

"Maybe it's the neighbor?" Kelly finally said.

I glanced at the house next door. Still and dark.

"Well, it's probably not the FBI," Deb said. "They usually don't travel by Harley."

"Someone," I said slowly, "needs to sneak up to the back of the house and look through the windows to see what's going on."

"Good idea," Kelly said.

"I'm pretty sure I left the curtains closed," Deb said.

"But you could probably see if anyone's moving," Kelly said.

We continued to sit and stare.

"Any volunteers?" Deb asked.

We all looked around at everything except one another.

I didn't know what frightened me more, finding out who was in the house, or dying of starvation, locked in the rental car for days, waiting to find out. "I'll go," I said.

I crept along the beach-access path, made a sharp left, then continued up to the deck steps. It was almost dark and my heart was pounding, but I calmed myself by watching the fog slowly roll in. I inched up the steps, then froze as I heard voices. Jason was out on the deck talking to someone, and the distinctive odor of pot was as thick as the fog.

That pissed me off, so I straightened up and looked around.

Sure enough, Jason was lounging on a deck chair, smoking a big old joint with, of all people, Liam.

"Hey!" I yelled, and felt a jolt of satisfaction as both men jumped up. "What the hell are you doing?"

Jason waved the joint at me. Liam grinned. "Well, now, Annie, I came by to make sure you ladies were all right, and look who I found?"

I leaned over the railing and yelled for everyone to come up. I folded my arms and turned back to Liam. "Where's the Mercedes?"

He shrugged. "I only drive that on special occasions."

Deb came bounding up onto the deck. She looked around, quickly assessed the situation, then went over and smacked Liam on the side of his head with her palm. "What kind of asshole are you?" she yelled.

Liam shrank back in his chair. "I just came by to make sure you were fine. I was worried about you."

"So, since we weren't home, you snuck around, saw Jason through a window, and thought you'd just invite yourself in?"

The look on Liam's face confirmed every one of Deb's words. But he was still fighting it out. "At least I know why you went through all that cloak-and-dagger business just to rent a car. That minivan of yours is hotter than a three-dollar pistol."

Jason took another hit and smiled lazily. "Listen, don't get your knickers in a twist. Liam was just being friendly."

I snatched the joint from Jason's hand and threw it out into the dunes. "Are you crazy?" I hissed. "You're out here getting high with a total stranger? What if he blabs about this around town, how he was getting high with the famous and kidnapped Jason Wilde? Ever think about that? We could all be in serious trouble here."

"Ah, take it easy. Liam is a good guy, aren't you, Liam?" Jason looked past Deb, as if trying to locate the joint in the darkness.

Liam smiled weakly, trying, no doubt, to look like a good guy. He was also looking at Kelly with a lovesick expression on his face.

"Hey, darlin', I missed you."

"Get inside," Kelly said between gritted teeth. "Both of you. Now."

The two men went into the house, and we all followed. Kelly shut the sliding doors with the conviction of a jailer. Deb tossed her bag on the kitchen table, then turned to face the men, hands on her hips, lips in a thin line.

"This situation has become extremely difficult, Jason. It's bad enough you have locked us into this ridiculous scheme of yours, but now Liam is involved. What are you going to do about it?"

Both men backed away and sat down abruptly on the couch.

Jason's jaw dropped open. "Me?"

"Yes, Jason. You," Deb snapped. "When we left this morning, all the drapes were drawn so that nobody could see you in here. Obviously, you opened them at some point, allowing Liam in on your little secret. Which was a very stupid move, by the way. Even though Liam was acting totally inappropriately by skulking around trying—"

"I was not skulking," Liam objected. "I knocked on the door and no one answered. I was just concerned."

Deb narrowed her eyes. "You're a born skulker," she spat. "And thanks to the prince of witless over here, you know a lot more than you should."

She turned her glare back to Jason. "This is entirely your problem. There is nothing we can do to prevent Liam from leaving and telling anyone he chooses what's going on, and it will go just as badly for you as it will for us. Figure this out, sonny boy."

I have to say, I almost felt sorry for Jason. Up until now, he'd had us all pretty much in the palm of his hand. Or at least he thought he did. To have Deb turn around with a full blast of Deb-ness must have been a shock to his system.

"Please, don't be mad," Jason said. He went all puppy eyes, and his beautiful body slumped and his head hung down . . .

"Jerk," Deb muttered. "We need to sort this through, one thing at a time. First, Liam." She fixed a cold and stony eye on him. "What are we going to do about you?"

Liam smiled. "Why do you need to do anything? Jason here explained it all."

Deb tightened her lips. "And Jason, you're perfectly fine with Liam here going about his normal business for the next few days, even though he could, at any moment, give away our little secret and get us all thrown in prison?"

Jason grinned broadly. "Liam's cool."

"How do you know?" I asked. "Just because he was willing to share his stash with you does not automatically make him a good guy. I know plenty of assholes who smoke pot."

Jason stopped grinning. "Well, I guess that's true." His brow puckered in fierce concentration. "What should we do?"

Deb sank into a chair across from the two men, who were still somewhat huddled together, like when zebras try to press themselves together to confuse a hunting lioness. She folded her arms across her chest and sat back, lifting her shoulders elaborately, then letting them slump. Liam looked sideways at Kelly.

"We could keep him here," Kelly suggested.

I looked at her. "He may not want to stay here for the rest of the week."

"I suppose we could always handcuff him to the bed frame," she said coolly.

"Darlin'," he sighed.

Jason arched his eyebrows. "You have handcuffs?" he asked.

Kelly shrugged. "If I did, I'd find better men to use them on than you."

Liam sighed again. "Ah, yes!"

"If we keep him here," I said, "he would be missed. It's not like he's some jobless vagrant who could drop off the face of the earth without a ripple."

"But if we turn him loose," Kelly said, "he could tell anyone."

"Here's the situation," Deb said. "Jason refuses to leave. If we call the police, he will accuse us of unlawful restraint or even kidnapping. But now, with Liam collaborating our story, we'll probably get off scot-free, and then Jason and slimy Artie will be the ones getting thrown in jail."

"Wait a minute," Liam said rather loudly.

We turned to look at him.

He swallowed. "I would not be in a position to collaborate anything."

Deb got right in his face. "Why not?"

Liam avoided Deb's gaze. He cleared his throat and stretched his neck from one side to the other. "Can't tell," he finally mumbled.

Kelly clapped her hands in obvious delight. "Then you really are in the Witness Protection Program?"

Liam turned white.

"Well, then, I guess we don't have to worry about him spilling the beans, right?" I said, grasping for any straw, no matter how tattered.

"Dude," Jason said.

My phone buzzed. It was a text from Andy. He could get away for an hour. Did I still feel like a pizza?

"Hey, everybody?" I said. "Listen, I know we need to sort this out, but can we take a short dinner break?"

Liam sat up. "Excellent idea. I'm starving."

Jason grinned slowly. "And I have *so* got the munchies."

Kelly looked over at me with a raised eyebrow. "Lover boy?"

I nodded.

Deb threw her hands up, silver rings flashing in the air. "Go. Meet your date, I guess. Nobody is going anywhere anytime soon." She fixed The Look of Death on Liam. "Right?"

Liam nodded.

I texted Andy back. I could meet him in fifteen minutes. I looked down at myself. I hadn't showered, I was not wearing a Class A or even Class B bra, and my eyes were getting crusty. I grabbed the rental-car keys off the table and ran out the door.

Brunetti's was kind of hard to find, tucked around a corner on Main Street. It was tiny, with only a few chairs at the counter, and fewer tables in the main room. The pizza there was prepared in an open kitchen, where you watched the cook make the pie in front of your very eyes, slide it into the wood-burning oven to bake, and then bring it out minutes later, crisp and delicious.

It was a must-visit for us ladies, and we would eat there at least once every year. Andy was obviously a man of impeccable taste.

He had saved me a seat at the counter. He was in a suit—dark gray with a subtle stripe.

He put down his menu. "I'm guessing you've eaten here before?"

I nodded and told him what I wanted—a thin-crust pizza topped with cheese, fig jam, fresh greens, and a balsamic glaze.

He looked at me out of the corner of his eye. "That's the closest pizza there is to a salad. You're not one of those constant dieters, are you?"

I made a face back at him. "Look at this body. I have no waist whatsoever. Do I look like I diet?"

He grinned. "You look fabulous."

No one had complimented me on my looks in years. I grinned back. "Keep it up, buddy. You're scoring points."

He was drinking water. I ordered a glass of wine.

"So, you're on day three—or is it four?—of your vacation. What have you done so far?" he asked.

Luckily, I had swallowed my first sip of wine, and there was nothing for me to spit out all over his nice suit.

"Sag Harbor," I said. "Lunch at that place on the dock, a few shops, a few drinks, and chowder for dinner." I thought it best to leave out the part about harboring an alleged kidnapping victim. "We've hit a few vineyards. Walked around a lot. We can't afford to buy anything, but it's good exercise."

"And the weather got better," he said.

Our pizzas arrived, and we spent a few minutes eating. I offered him a bite of mine. He looked skeptical, took a bite, and closed his eyes and sighed.

"That's pretty amazing for salad," he said.

We ate in silence. It was a happy silence. We looked at each other a lot and smiled. I was so friggin' happy, I felt like a sixteen-year-old on a first-ever date. He finished his entire pizza. I had the few pieces left of mine put in a takeaway box.

I could not look away from his eyes. Not when he lowered his glass, not when he took my wineglass from my hand and set it on the counter. And then I had to close my eyes.

Because he kissed me.

I kissed him back.

And if we hadn't been sitting on two separate stools, who knows what would have happened.

After we pulled away, he looked serious, watching the pizza oven intently.

"Are you sure you're not married?" he asked.

"Of course I'm not married. I told you I was divorced."

"And you're not on leave from a psych ward?"

"Maybe I should be, but I'm not. What's going on?"

"I want to make sure I'm not setting myself up for a big fall," he said.

"Andy?"

He finally looked at me. "Please don't be the woman who breaks my heart," he said.

"Why would I want to do that?"

"You wouldn't want to, but you could. I've never fallen so fast or so hard in my life, and I'm afraid you're going to turn out to be a nutcase or a compulsive liar or a wanted criminal."

My heart was in my throat. Because he said he had fallen for me. And also because, technically speaking, I *was* a wanted criminal.

"I know how you feel," I told him, my voice cracking. "Listen, I'm usually not like this. At all. I'm running into this full-speed ahead, and I'm usually cautious and slow and spend most of my time overthinking everything. With you, I feel like I'm not thinking much at all. Just doing. So, like, you could just as easily break my heart, you know?"

He smiled. "That's reassuring, I guess. I have to get back. We'd better go."

We walked out to the street and stood by his car.

"I'm late and am going to get reamed for it. When can I see you again?"

"Whenever you want. Since you live so close, we could probably take morning walks together."

He laughed. "I don't live close. I just happen to be working on Dune Road."

I leaned against his car. "Lucky for us. Since I told you what I do for a living, it's your turn. Wearing a suit? I'll go with very neat landscaper."

He made a face. "If you must know, I'm with the FBI. Supervising Special Agent Andrew Sean Mooney. I'm working the Jason Wilde kidnapping. His rental house is on Dune Road, and since that's where the ransom note was sent, we've set up shop there."

Thank God it was dark, because I'm sure my face underwent several changes of color and expression. "Oh?" I managed to croak.

He opened the car door. "It's a very good thing I saw you at John Scott's. I know that your third friend isn't a skinny white chick with purple hair. Otherwise, you could be on the top of my suspect list."

"Oh?"

He kissed me lightly, got in his car, and then drove away.

I stood there in the fog and the mist, my mouth hanging open.

Oh.

Oh, my God.

I drove slowly back to the house. What on earth was I going to do? What was I going to tell everyone? *Should* I tell everyone? Of course I should. After all, I was now sleeping with the enemy. Well, not sleeping, exactly. I was *wanting* to sleep with the enemy. Which seemed like the same thing.

Why me? Why such amazing bad luck? Here was Andrew Sean Mooney—smart, funny, handsome, sexy, a great kisser, and he liked his home fries extra crispy, just like I did. When I looked at him, I wanted to immediately pucker up. Now, maybe it was a purely physiological reaction, since I hadn't had sex in so long, but I didn't think so.

I really liked this man.

And he was leaving me to go to work and look for me, so I could be questioned for possibly committing a federal offense.

I opened the door of 461 Dune Road slowly. Everyone was there, watching TV.

It was quite the cozy scene. Kelly and Liam were side by side on the couch, her head against his shoulder. Jason was sprawled on one chair, a beer in his hand, and Deb was tucked in the corner, reading on her Kindle. Everyone looked up as I walked in.

Jason grinned. "Hey, you have leftovers? Great. Can I have a peek? I'm still hungry."

Deb clucked like a mother hen. "Jason, you had two bowls of chowder and that huge sandwich. How can you be hungry?"

He shrugged. "What can I say? Munchies, man." He bounded off the chair and crossed the room, grabbing my pizza box and looking hopefully inside.

Kelly looked back over her shoulder. "Have fun?"

I had to clear my throat. "Yes. Ah, listen—"

"Wait. Here comes the news," Liam said. He reached for the remote. "It's good to know what your enemy is planning."

On the screen was a stern-looking man in a dark suit, standing behind a podium. The caption indicated that the FBI had issued a statement in the kidnapping of Jason Wilde earlier that evening. I took a few steps closer.

". . . and because of the lack of further communication from the kidnappers, aside from the original note, we are going to have to reassess our next move."

As he continued, the camera pulled back. Behind him, in dark suits, heads bowed and hands clasped solemnly, were several other men, presumably agents. And there, right at the end, stood a very tall, very attractive, and decidedly familiar-looking man.

Kelly frowned. "That guy on the end?"

Deb looked up. "The tall one? Well, now, that is one hot-looking G-man.

Kelly squinted at the screen. "Is it just me, or does he look familiar?"

Deb tilted her head. "Yes. He does. Annie?"

They all looked at me. I cleared my throat.

"That would be Andy."

Deb arched her eyebrows. Kelly's shoulders slumped.

Jason looked over. "Andy?"

I nodded. "Yes. Andy. Who I just ate pizza with."

Jason grinned. "So, you're boning a fed?"

"My, my," Liam cackled. "Now, this *is* getting interesting."

"I am not," I explained quietly, "boning anyone."

Jason raised an eyebrow. "Well, maybe you should be. Then you wouldn't be so cranky all the time."

"I'm not cranky all the time!" I yelled. I glanced at Kelly and Deb. They had the same 'Are you kidding?' look on their faces.

I brought my voice down to a more acceptable level. "I just found out now. Like, ten minutes ago. Andy *happens* to be working on Jason's case."

I waited for a bolt of lightning to come through the ceiling, or at least an ominous crack of thunder off in the distance. Nothing. The candles didn't even sputter.

"Does he know who you are?" Kelly asked at last.

"Does he know I'm a fiftysomething divorcée from Hopewell, New Jersey? Yes. Does he know I'm housemates with Jason Wilde, currently the subject of a federal manhunt? No."

"I think I need more wine," Deb muttered.

"I didn't know what to do," I told them. "I really like this guy. It's not his fault he's with the FBI."

Liam looked thoughtful. "I know Andy. He's a lovely chap. Really. But he takes his job very seriously. And he's not just a field agent. He's, like, in charge of things. Big things. He runs the agency office out in Melville."

Deb scowled at him. "And do you know him in a *professional* capacity?"

Liam shrugged. "Hey, I've lived here a long time, and he's a regular. You meet people, you know?"

"Of course," Kelly said. Her face had softened just a little. "That makes perfect sense."

Liam beamed.

"This may work to our advantage," Kelly said. "Maybe Ann could explain the situation to him, and he could figure out a way to solve everything."

Liam shook his head. "Ladies, you are in—as we say on the wrong side of the law—deep doo-doo. At this point, you are collaborators. Or coconspirators. Or accomplices. Something like that."

"Are you trying to impress us with your legal expertise?" Deb asked.

He smirked. "I may not be a legal eagle, but I know a shit storm when I see it. And I don't think Andy would be in any position to help you out, even if he does carry some authority. This is not some local case. The branch office in New York City has stepped in. This is too big."

Jason, chewing pizza, nodded modestly.

"Well, the bottom line is that I think we can trust Liam," Kelly said.

I looked at her skeptically. "Oh?"

"After all, if he blabs to anyone, he could very well end up on national TV," Deb said. "He's right. This is big."

Liam turned slightly pale again.

Kelly tapped his knee. "Seriously? Witness Protection? Because we just made that up. Our other option was that you were on the run from the Boston mob."

Liam cleared his throat. "I suppose I should be flattered that you all have spent so much time imagining my life."

"We're from a sleepy little town in New Jersey," Deb said. "Whatever happens on vacation is usually the most excitement we see."

He grinned. "Well, you are certainly getting your fair share on this trip," he said.

Kelly tapped his knee again. "So, Deb is right? We can trust you, because if you open your big mouth, all sorts of hell will descend upon you?"

He stopped grinning and swallowed hard. "Possibly."

"Good." She turned to me. "Now. What are we going to do about Andy?"

"I really like him," I said. "We're supposed to see each other again."

"Well, at least we don't have to worry about him murdering you and hiding your body," Deb said. "Although, if he did, he'd probably do a *very* good job."

"He is not going to hide my body anywhere," I said.

Kelly looked at me with a smile. "Of course he's not."

"But how do you know," Jason said, "that you won't spill your guts in a moment of, ah, high passion?"

I raised both eyebrows. "High passion?"

Jason shrugged. "Chicks always tell me crazy stuff after, well, you know. It's like they want you to know their deepest secret, so, like, you'll never leave them."

"You," Kelly said, "need to stop sleeping with stupid little girls, and try a grown woman for once."

"First of all, there will be no 'high passion,'" I told him. "And if there is, I would not automatically blurt out anything. Kelly's right. Find yourself a real woman."

Jason shrugged again. "Real, fake, doesn't matter to me. I'm an equal-opportunity lover."

"That sounds cool," Kelly said, "but it's not."

"How old are you again?" Deb asked. "Equal-opportunity boy?"

Jason blushed even deeper. "Forty-seven."

Liam hooted. "Lookin' good, boyo."

Liam was right. Even without makeup and lighting, all the things that made him so handsome on-screen, he looked terrific. He took *very* good care of himself.

"And *how* old is your girlfriend?" Deb continued.

"Twenty-three."

Kelly made a face. "Ew."

I shuddered. "Yeah. Well, too bad you chased Tina away. At least she was in the same age bracket."

Jason frowned. "I'm sure you know this, but your friend Tina is a little odd."

Deb rolled her eyes. "Ya think? The only reason she came out here with us was to *run into* you. So she finds your favorite bar, flirts with the bartender for information, drags us out in the middle of the night so we can hang out while she sits and waits for you. Which is how you ended up here in the first place. And then she runs off without a word and leaves us with all her toilet paper. And her dog. Odd does not begin to cover it."

"If she hadn't come on so strong, she might have had a chance," Jason said. "She's smart and very independent. She's also probably got a hundred different crackpot things wrong with her, but that's because her mind is going in a hundred different directions at once. Women like her scare the hell out of me. Seriously. I don't care how sexy they are, I run in the opposite direction every time I see one coming. But I bet when she's not being a total nutcase, she's a blast."

Deb shook her head and chuckled. "You are so right about her, Jason. You're getting a little scary about your way of figuring people out, you know?"

Kelly stood up and ran her hand through her hair. "So, I guess we just sit tight for now?"

Liam cleared his throat. "The FBI will be doing a house-to-house. Soon. They've probably already started."

Kelly frowned. "So?"

"So," Liam said, "you have a silver minivan with Jersey plates parked out front."

Deb said something nasty. Kelly sat back down.

"We might as well just hoist a great big flag saying **KIDNAPPED GUY HERE**," I said.

"Just switch the plates," Jason said, stretching. "You know, what? I'm kinda tired. See you all in the morning."

"What do you mean?" Kelly asked. "Switch the plates?"

"Simple," Jason said. "The rental car has New York plates, right? They're looking for a minivan with Jersey plates, so just switch the two sets of plates. That way, the cops are fooled into passing right by."

We all turned as one to look at him.

"That's brilliant," Kelly said.

Jason grinned. "Yeah. We just shot that for the show."

"That explains it," Deb muttered. "I knew that was too good an idea for—"

"Deb, let's just be thankful for a solution, no matter where it came from," I said.

"Liam, have you got a screwdriver?" Kelly asked. "Do you need a flashlight?"

"I've got tools in my car," he said, "but nothing on the bike. Is there something here? And I'll need someone to hold the flashlight."

Deb rummaged through a junk drawer in the kitchen, then held up a screwdriver and a small LED flashlight. "You're up, Jason," she said.

"Me? Why me?"

"Because," Deb said, as sweetly as possible, for her, "you're the reason we're in this mess in the first place."

"But what if somebody sees me?" Jason argued, somewhat reasonably.

Deb looked over the top of her glasses. "You mean someone wearing night goggles? Or someone who happens to have night vision as their superpower?"

Kelly jumped up. "Never mind, Jason. I'll go."

Liam beamed. "Darlin'."

Chapter Eight

Andy did not text me that night. Of course he didn't. He was too busy trying to find the three crazed women who'd stolen Jason Wilde.

I did not sleep well. Besides Andy and Jason, I kept thinking about Kelly and Deb. Were they as scared as I was? Kelly was always grace under stress. Deb just plowed through everything. It was part of her personality, not just her job. But I had never been the one to take the lead in an emergency, and to my mind, being wanted for kidnapping, even if the kidnapping never really happened, constituted an emergency.

My desire to solve this situation as quickly as possible was in direct conflict with my natural inclination to find a safe corner somewhere and let somebody else do the work.

The sun was shining when I woke up, and I chose to take that as a positive sign. After all, we were going to try to find Artie Sherman and talk him into taking Jason Wilde off our hands, as well as figuring out a story that would take the FBI off our trail.

We were discussing strategy around the breakfast table.

"I think we should appeal to his better nature," I suggested. "I'm sure once we explain how scared we are, Artie will take pity on us."

Deb looked at me, shaking her head. "Are you kidding? I bet this Artie guy is desperate. Look at it: Jason is on the brink of losing his job, which means Artie's percentage will dry up to nothing. He's right about one thing—the publicity is priceless. Hell, Jason will probably be a media darling for months to come. If Artie has any brains at all, he'll make a ton of money off this whole thing."

"Well, I'm pretty sure Artie *is* the brains." Kelly said. "Because, as much as I love Jason, I don't think he's too bright."

I stared at her. "You love Jason? When did that happen? Look at the position he's put us in."

Kelly looked embarrassed. "I know. And I don't mean *love* love. But there's something very, I don't know, sweet about him. Last night, he pulled me aside to tell me he thought Liam was a good guy."

"Of course he thinks Liam is a good guy," I said. "They got high together. They'll be friends for life. That's the male equivalent of shoe shopping at the outlets on Memorial Day." I looked at Deb. "Right?"

She made a small face. "I think he's kind of lovable, for a white guy. And you know, he's one of those people who are really interested in, I don't know, your soul. Yes, that's it. He really wants to know you and see that you're happy."

"Then why is he so stubborn about making us a part of this crazy scheme if he knows we're miserable about it?" I asked.

"Well," Deb said, "he's being a jerk about this, but he's obviously used to doing what he's told. It's not his fault."

"Yes, it is," I said. My voice may have risen a decibel or three. "This whole thing is his fault. He's not just a jerk—he's a selfish, thoughtless, and totally irresponsible jerk. And if the FBI knocks on our door and we all end up going to jail, are you still going to think he's lovable?"

I looked up to see Jason standing there, looking fairly miserable.

"You really think I'm an irresponsible jerk?" he asked.

I leaned back in my chair. "Let's face it, Jason, your whole attitude about this has been rather selfish. All you can think about is publicity, when there's a whole other side to this that involves the police and the Feds and the possibility of real jail time."

"I would never let you go to jail," he said. "I'd make sure to straighten everything out in the end."

"But Jason," I argued, "even if we're not actually breaking the law, keeping quiet about all this is bound to get us into trouble. And it's not going to be forgotten just because you say, 'Oops, it was all a joke.'"

Deb had opened her mouth to speak when there was a knock at the door.

Jason froze for a moment and then started to back out of the kitchen. Kelly pulled on his arm. "Stay in the bedroom," she whispered. "Close the door and wait by the sliders. If someone turns the knob, run like hell out to the beach."

He nodded and disappeared around the corner.

Deb flexed her shoulders and opened the door, and sure enough, two dark-suited men stood there, one handsome and very Waspish, the other equally handsome and African American, looking polite and very official.

The Denzel Washington clone held out a badge and spoke. "I'm Agent Geller. Is the owner available?"

Muffy launched herself off the living-room couch and came racing in, teeth bared, looking like an overprotective rat. Deb reached down and scooped her up before the ritual leg humping could begin.

"No, sorry," she said. Her face softened, and her smile became almost flirtatious. "I'm Deborah Esposito. We're actually renting the house for the week. You're FBI? I suppose you're here about that poor actor. What's his name?" Deb's voice practically dripped with sweetness.

"Jason Wilde," Agent Geller said. "Yes. We're just checking to see if anyone saw anything that might be of use."

The other agent was looking at Kelly. Did I mention she was tall, blonde . . . ?

Kelly leaned forward and spoke to Deb. Rapidly. In French. I looked downward to hide the fact that my jaw dropped open. Deb answered. Also in French.

"You must excuse Chloe," Deb said to Agent Geller. "She actually finds this very exciting."

Kelly-Chloe flashed a million-dollar smile.

"Is the minivan yours? We noticed it's a rental," Agent Geller said.

"You can tell?" I asked.

The other agent nodded. "From the plates."

Deb smiled. "Yes. Well. Annie here, she lives in Hopewell. That's in New Jersey. She drove in alone. Chloe and I took the train from Queens. I always rent something out here. My husband and I have only the one car, you see."

Agent Geller nodded and looked directly at Kelly. "And, ah, Chloe?"

"My cousin," Deb said quickly, then squeezed her eyes shut tightly, realizing how implausible that seemed. "That is . . . my husband's cousin, just visiting. From France."

I looked up and managed a smile, hoping they wouldn't notice my knees knocking together. Kelly just tilted her head and looked Parisian.

Agent Geller nodded. "And have any of you seen any strange activity out here?"

Deb cleared her throat. "To be honest, we've spent most of our time shopping. We haven't actually been home, except at night. That actor, does he live around here?"

He nodded again. "Yes, just down the road, as a matter of fact." He reached in his pocket and handed Deb his card. "If you see or hear anything odd, please call us?"

Deb clasped the card to her breast. "Of course. Anything to help that poor young man."

The other agent was still looking at Kelly. Maybe, at this point, he was just admiring the view. They both nodded and walked down the steps.

Deb shut the door behind them, leaned against it, and closed her eyes. "I don't think I could ever go through something like that again. The FBI. Right. Here."

Kelly let out a long, shaky laugh. "Thank God you know French."

"I don't," Deb said, tossing Muffy to the ground. "That was just a line from a movie I happened to remember."

I think I'd been holding my breath. This was why I'd never be the one leading the charge. I might be good at planning, but when it came to execution, I froze like the cowardly lion I was at heart. I threw my arms around Deb and hugged her. "You were amazing. I would have stammered us right into Alcatraz."

Deb pushed me away and waved her hands. "Is Alcatraz even a thing anymore? You watch too many old movies, Annie." She walked over to the sliding glass doors. "Okay, enough with the cloak-and-dagger crap. I'm not spending the whole vacation dealing with Jason Wilde's kidnapping. Today would be a good beach day. The sun is actually shining, and the wind is down. This will probably be the best day we get all week."

We all looked out over the dunes. Yes, a beach day, to remind us why we came all the way out here in the first place.

The beach at the Hamptons was different from other beaches I'd been to. I know—same ocean, right? Maybe. It didn't just smell different; the waves were quiet, the beaches wide and clean, and the light was amazing. Beach days did not mean frolicking in the waves. The water was too cold, for one thing. Beach days at Dune Road meant stretched out on tattered blankets, reading in the warm sun and drinking wine from a thermos, talking, and napping the afternoon away.

"Kelly and I should be back here fairly early. We can spend the afternoon?" I said hopefully. "We'll get food on our way back."

Deb nodded reluctantly, and Kelly and I were out of the house in less than thirty minutes.

I glanced over at Kelly. "You and Liam seemed very comfortable last night. After you reamed him a new one, that is."

I expected her to start to blush, but she just grinned. "All the times we had spent flirting with each other, it was so easy for me because I was still married. So it wasn't, like, the real thing. I was kind of terrified of what would happen this year, because, now that I'm divorced, it could be the real thing. But it still felt nice and relaxed and, well, playful. We really do get along. I really do like him. And that chemistry is, well, real." Her grin got broader. "You weren't the only one to get a little action last night."

"Well, go you," I said, and I turned the car out onto Dune Road.

It was turning into a gorgeous day. We drove around miles of backstreets, slowing down past the beautiful homes. Most of them were behind perfectly trimmed walls of boxwood, but occasionally you could glimpse more than a shingled roof or a flash of gunite pool. Everything was perfectly green and manicured.

"I want to be rich," Kelly said wistfully.

"Me too. Can you imagine waking up every day and looking out over lawn and beach?"

She shook her head. "And most of these people don't even live here all the time. I'd never leave."

We made it back to Mike's bar by ten thirty. The parking lot wasn't as crowded, but the car-to-motorcycle ratio looked about the same.

"Are you ready?" I asked. I could feel my heart start to beat a little faster.

She nodded. "How about you? I know this must be really hard for you."

"What, this? Driving out here and risking my future on the possibility we can convince some cranky old man to do the right thing? Piece of cake."

She looked at me, frowning. "Just the driving-out-here part. Usually you're the planner, not the doer."

"Believe it or not, it's getting easier. I think I'm loosening up."

"Really?"

"Hey, I let Andy take a bite out of my pizza."

"Right," she said, and once again we headed for the bar.

Kelly breezed in, quickly found the bartender, and raised her eyebrows. He shook his head. She nodded, then found the farthest table from the door and sat.

The bartender hurried over. "I made a fresh pot of coffee for you," he whispered.

I glanced around. Was that supposed to be a secret?

Kelly pushed back her hair in a very dramatic gesture. "You're too kind," she purred. The bartender hurried off and returned with a tray with two steaming cups, and well as milk and sugar.

The coffee was actually quite good, even though he forgot spoons and I had to stir in my sugar with a Bic pen from my purse.

Kelly was on her phone, of course. I didn't know what she was looking at, or for, but I kept my eye fixed on the front door. I knew what Artie looked like, of course. He'd been easy to find on the Internet. But when he finally came through the door, it was obvious that his posted picture was several years old. Or maybe the stress of committing an act of fraud had taken a real toll.

He was short and very thin. He was dressed in dark-gray slacks and an oversize polo shirt. He had his phone to his ear as he came in and went straight to the bar. The bartender glanced at us, then poured what was obviously Artie's regular—a shot of something.

Kelly squared her shoulders and waved her hand in the air. "Artie? There you are, you naughty man. I can't believe you stood me up yesterday."

I had to hand it to her—it was exactly the right thing to say. He glanced over his shoulder at us and frowned, but put his phone away, downed his shot, and came over to our little corner.

"Do I know you ladies?" he asked politely. His voice was very soft and had the ring of Brooklyn about it.

Kelly patted the seat next to her. "Have a seat, please. We need to talk."

I looked around. I hadn't recognized any of the faces in the semi-darkness, but then, I could barely see them. I assumed it was the same crowd as yesterday afternoon, though, since no one paid any attention to us, when yesterday our arrival had caused a major stir.

Artie sat. He was still polite. "Talk about what?"

Kelly reached out and put her hand on his wrist. Then tightened her grip. "About Jason."

Artie's face fell. "Who are you?" he asked hoarsely.

"We're the ones who are playing host to Jason," Kelly said, a smile on her face but her voice like steel. "We also know who sent the ransom note. And we know that Jason was about to be written out of the show. They say that knowledge is power. If that's true, we are very powerful people. So you'd better listen to us very carefully."

Artie looked to be over sixty years old, and a fairly unhealthy sixty at that. He was pale, and his lips were dry and cracked. He kept blinking rapidly behind very thick glasses. He looked just the opposite of how the manager of a hot television star should look. But then, Jason wasn't so hot anymore. At Kelly's words, Artie turned an even pastier shade of white. I feared for his blood pressure.

"Listen," he said, his voice low, "Jason is a great kid. He's a bundle of talent. He's just a bit high-strung and is going through a rough patch. This kidnapping thing could turn his career around."

Kelly was still smiling. "First of all, Jason is not a kid. He's an adult. Second, he is not a bundle of talent. He may be the worst actor in the entire state of New York, which is saying something, believe me. And if any of us gave a rat's ass about his career, that all might be relevant. But we don't. You need to come and get him. We want him out. Today. Or would you rather we drop him off?" Gosh, she was masterful. Her voice was even and totally devoid of emotion. Just like the guy who left all those messages for Mr. Phelps on *Mission: Impossible*.

Artie leaned forward with pleading eyes. "Please. Leo and I have a lot riding on this. *Everything* is riding on this. Just a few more days."

Kelly leaned forward. "Listen to me. Jason is a terrible hostage. He eats a lot and wants to drink all our beer, and we found him getting high on our deck. We like him. At least I do. He really is a lovely man. But we don't want him anymore. Get. Him. Out."

"I'm in a crummy hotel room," he whined. "I can't bring him there."

"Then get another hotel room," Kelly said. "Or send him over to Leo's."

"Leo is . . . no. I can't send him to Leo. Leo is the moneyman. He doesn't love Jason the way I do. I can't send him anywhere. Someone will recognize him."

"We'll buy him sunglasses," Kelly said. "Besides, no one is going to expect to see him roaming the street. He's supposed to be locked up in a storage unit somewhere. We'll get him wherever you say, no problem."

"But what would I do with him?"

"The same thing we're doing with him," I snapped. "Feed him, keep the television on, and make sure he doesn't wander out and run into anybody. Come on, Artie. This whole kidnapping idea was yours. Take a little responsibility here, okay?"

He shook his head wildly. "This was not my idea. It was Leo's idea. I told him it was crazy. When Jason didn't come home, I figured he was just shacking up with somebody, you know? I mean he was right down the street. What trouble could he get into? But Leo, well, Leo came up with the kidnapping idea. We couldn't afford to have Jason lose his contract, and after all the publicity, we'd be able to sign him to a much better deal. My brother is really good with the numbers, not so much with the common sense."

"Wait a minute," I said. "How did you know Jason was just down the street?"

Artie looked slightly ashamed. "We have a GPS thing on his phone. The kid wanders a lot, especially with the women. We just keep tabs on him is all."

"Really?" I shook my head. "You might as well just microchip the guy."

"Listen, ladies, Jason is the only client we have left. Have pity on an old man and his dreams?"

Kelly leaned toward him. "No pity here, Artie, for you or your dreams. We want Jason gone."

Poor Artie. He looked positively stricken. He actually buried his face in his hands. Kelly and I exchanged smug glances. We had him.

He suddenly raised his head, a new man. "Five million dollars?" He was yelling. "I don't have five million dollars!"

Uh-oh.

He stood up. He was still yelling. "I need more time. Don't kill him, please!"

That dirty little . . .

Kelly and I looked at each other and stood up very calmly. Maybe, I thought, no one would notice.

I looked around. Every single person in the bar was staring at us. My mouth felt dry.

Kelly smiled weakly and waved at the looky-loos in the bar. "We're good," she called faintly. "Really."

Artie made a strangled noise. "What?" he croaked. "A gun?" I turned to look at him, and he was clutching his chest. His eyes met mine, and then he pitched forward onto the table, knocking coffee cups and sugar packets everywhere.

Kelly and I were out of there like a shot. As I hurried through the door, I could hear noises behind me, feet shuffling, the scraping of chairs. I was afraid to look back. I jumped into the Prius, praying it would take off like a rocket when I hit the gas. It did, and I floored it, throwing up gravel as we sped by the various bar patrons who were tumbling out the front door.

Kelly was swearing a hot streak, using words in combinations I'd never heard before.

"We are so screwed," I said, my voice shaking. "I hope no one is following us." I kept looking in the rearview mirror, waiting for a fleet of motorcycles to appear. So far, so good.

"That miserable—" Kelly began.

"We killed him," I wailed. I tightened my grip on the steering wheel to steady my nerves.

"I don't think so," Kelly said. "He was just giving us a chance to get out of there."

"What?"

"Think about it. He wants this to drag on for as long as possible. If someone had grabbed us and turned us over to the police, everything would be over. And it would not end well."

I was gripping the steering wheel so tightly I thought my knuckles would break. "Do you think? So, we didn't kill him?"

"Nope," Kelly said. "Now he and Leo have another chapter."

I took a deep breath. Now that the fight-or-flight reflex had quieted, my brain was starting to settle back into a logical place. "You're right. That FBI guy said they had to reassess. We just gave them more clues. We just put the kidnappers out there, soliciting ransom money in broad daylight. So, actually, that was pretty brilliant. But now we could be in real trouble." I was concentrating, making sure I didn't go over the speed limit. The last thing we needed was to be pulled over for speeding.

"What do you mean?" Kelly asked.

"I mean that now it's not just our word against Jason's. Now we have Artie, who will undoubtedly tell the FBI all sorts of crazy things. And now, people know what we look like. We can be identified. And fingerprints. Oh, God, we left fingerprints behind."

"Have you ever been fingerprinted for anything?" she asked.

"Nope. Have you?"

"My Realtor's license."

"Oh, crap. Now they can find us. Kelly, they'll track us down like dogs."

"No, Annie, calm down. Artie fell on the table. The coffee cups hit the floor. I heard them. Maybe they're too broken."

I glanced at Kelly. She was nodding, a very wide smile on her face. "Yeah?"

"Yeah. Or if they're not, maybe the bartender will have cleaned everything up before the police arrive. Once something goes through the dishwasher, fingerprints are gone, right?"

Was she kidding? I couldn't imagine the bartender cleaning up anything short of a bleeding corpse. As for a dishwasher, there was probably a one-legged guy named Mort who did the cleaning up with a bucket and an old diaper. "Absolutely."

She leaned back in the seat. "Okay. So. We're fine there."

"But people saw us. All those men."

"Who were all drinking at eleven in the morning in a badly lit bar," Kelly said. "And did you get a look at Artie's glasses? I bet he couldn't pick us out of a lineup even if we were the only women. Besides, he can't afford for us to be found, remember? He'll probably send the police after two Asian teenagers with tattoos."

"You think?" I asked.

"I know," she said, still smiling. I got the distinct impression that she was enjoying the whole situation just a little too much.

We drove. On our way home, we stopped to pick up more chowder, sandwich meat and fresh bread, and another cherry pie. I had piled my hair on top of my head and kept my sunglasses on, thinking that my next step would be a fake mustache and a green wig, but the woman at the farm stand barely looked up at me.

I was getting the food out of the backseat when Deb came rushing down the steps.

"What did you do?" If it was possible to shriek in a whisper, that's what she sounded like.

Kelly's face fell. "What?"

Deb hustled us back up the stairs.

The news was on.

Of course it was.

And there was breaking news in the Jason Wilde case.

Of course there was.

It seemed as though Arthur Sherman, sixty-five, partner in the Sherman & Associates Talent Group and manager to kidnapped actor Jason Wilde, had been approached by two of the kidnappers in a local bar. They demanded five million in ransom to be delivered in three days. They apparently had a gun. Sherman had collapsed while trying to detain one of the kidnappers, and was under observation at a local hospital. Police had questioned eyewitnesses on the scene and were now looking for a blonde actress, midforties, possibly named Kelly, and her partner, a shorter brunette, somewhat older. Both women, according to the FBI, were to be considered armed and dangerous.

Chapter Nine

"Armed?" Deb croaked. "And dangerous?"

Jason was sitting on the couch, obviously upset. "What did you do to Artie?"

Kelly glared at him. "We told him to come and get you because we were tired of this whole ridiculous situation. That's what we did to Artie. He took it upon himself to create a scene and throw himself across a table."

"How did you find him anyway?" Jason asked. He hadn't shaved in a few days, which only added to his good looks, but made him seem a bit dangerous.

Deb had her Kindle in her hand. She flung it onto the chair as she waved her hands wildly. "Jason, it doesn't matter. What matters is that you have to leave here. We are now seriously in danger of being found out, which means we are going to jail unless something changes right now. This has to stop." She put her hands on either side of her head and took a deep breath. "Tonight we'll take you out to Montauk. Late. We can drop you off in the dunes somewhere." She looked hard at him. "Whatever story you make up is all up to you, Jason. Just remember that you're in as much trouble about this as we are."

Jason folded his arms across his chest and shook his head. "No. Not until Artie tells me to."

"Jason," Kelly pleaded, tugging her hair. "think about this. Artie is in the hospital. How is he going to be able to tell you anything?"

He lifted his chin. "Then I'll wait for Leo. Leo will know how to find me."

"How?" Kelly asked. "They're both probably being watched. How would either of them get a message to you? Skywriting?"

Jason frowned. "I guess you're right, but—"

"No buts! We can't afford to wait!" I yelled. "Don't you get it? It's bad enough that even if you do turn up tomorrow, this case will still be investigated. Maybe forever. We are all in danger. And the longer you're here, the worse it will get. I do not want to go to prison. Do you?"

Jason looked uncomfortable. He frowned, like he was thinking hard. He made a few faces. Then his arms dropped to his side. "I don't know what to do," he finally said.

"I know you don't," Deb said. "Knowing, in general, is not your strong suit. Not about this kind of stuff, anyway. Why is that, Jason? You are so great about other people. Why are you so incapable of making decisions about yourself?"

His frown grew deeper. Obviously, he was really giving this a lot of consideration. He finally nodded, almost to himself.

"I'm not a good actor," he said. "I know that. I'm fine when I can just be myself. I'm great at that, but anything else . . . lots of actors are insecure, you know? But I *know* I don't have much talent. Artie has been with me from the beginning. He knows, and he has always found me work. He's the reason I have any career at all. So I do whatever he says. Without question. He's the only person in the world whose interests are exactly like mine." He ran a hand through his hair, tousling it perfectly. "When it comes to figuring out my own life, especially my career, I'm kind of an idiot."

Deb's expression softened. "*Idiot* is a strong word. Kind of. We'll figure it all out for you. We're going out to the beach. We'll talk it over, and by the time we get back, it will all be planned out. I promise."

He was looking at her without the least bit of confidence. "Yeah?"

She nodded. "Yeah." She turned to us. "Right, ladies?"

I nodded, feeling exhausted. I went out on the deck and checked my phone. Four texts from Andy. The first, a row of emoticons, all smiley faces. The next was Tonite??? The third, Shit. The fourth, Watch TV and you'll know why I can't talk.

He couldn't talk because he was talking to Artie. Or to all those bar patrons, who were giving detailed descriptions of the lesbian couple who had shown up the previous day. Would there be an artist's rendering? Would my face, carefully sketched in charcoal, be plastered all over national television?

"It's a beach day, girls," Deb said. She'd come out and was standing beside me. "Let's go get some sun."

"Deb," I said, "we're all over the news right now. Don't you think lying out on a public beach is a bit risky?"

Deb put her hands on her hips. "Listen, I've been dreaming about that beach for months. Kelly, do something with that blonde hair of yours. And if anyone walks by, start talking in French again. Lucky for you all, you've got the curvy black girl to throw the Feds off the scent."

"We need to figure out a plan," I said.

She nodded. "Yes, Annie, and you are the best we've got. So you need to relax and let that brain of yours go to work."

I headed up to my room, put on my bathing suit, hid my hair under a floppy hat, grabbed a towel, and then went downstairs.

We brought our lunch, picnic style, down the short path to the beach. It was midseventies, there was no wind, and the water was as calm as a lake. Kelly had wrapped her hair in a scarf, which, on her, looked like an exotic turban. On me, it would have looked like a babushka. We spread a quilt and sat and ate in silence. We made sandwiches on crusty bread, and we drank lots of wine. We didn't talk. We stretched out in the sun, watching the water.

I started thinking about how I could leave the country, make my way down to a Caribbean island (one without an extradition treaty with the United States), and live alone, high in a mountain cabin, eating bananas and goat meat. I didn't think I'd like living in isolation, so I imagined Deb and Kelly with me, and it was a bit better, but I thought we'd end up driving one another crazy.

Then I figured out how I could use my deceased mother's Social Security number and live in a small town in West Texas, working in a bar, making martinis and living on tips.

The more I thought about that scenario, the less attractive it sounded. My imagination took a turn there for a moment, and I pictured myself on the run with a notorious motorcycle gang after being kidnapped for my unrivaled cocktail-making skills.

So I went straight for the hard stuff, where Deb, Kelly, and I all ended up in the same federal prison, maybe that one down in West Virginia where Martha Stewart had taught everyone how to crochet.

Hmm.

I knew that if I thought about it long enough, I'd figure a way out. Then I could imagine a life with Andy.

He was a good man, I knew. He was the kind of man I could love. He was definitely the kind of man I could have wild monkey sex with. There was a future there. Maybe. If he wasn't forced, at some point in our relationship, to arrest me.

But.

Could we sustain a long-distance relationship? Did I want to? It's not that I had any *real* commitment issues, but I didn't even have a cat because I was afraid a pet would cause some sort of ripple in my life. If I was nervous about having to accommodate a cat, how was I going to manage a real man?

And it wasn't like I was lazy or anything. I wouldn't mind working more nights to have weekends free. I'd have no trouble shaving my legs more than once a week, or even driving out to the Hamptons to see him.

The problem was, I was used to things the way they were. I *liked* things the way they were. And although I might daydream about love and adventure, so far the adventure part was proving way more than I could handle. What was going to happen with love?

But I allowed my mind to wander into a happy place. Maybe I'd just move out here and spend my days gazing at the ocean, waiting for Andy to come home to grilled steaks and wine. I was planning our retirement home in the Hamptons when reality bit me in the butt.

"What should we do?" Kelly asked.

"We could just pack up and go home," Deb said. "Leave him to sort out this mess by himself."

Kelly shook her head. "We are in too deep now. And I'm not sure Jason is smart enough to sort this out. We need him to be found."

We watched the water some more. Thinking about Andy was good inspiration. I was actually forming an idea.

"Listen."

They all turned to me.

"That patch," I said. "You know, for his back? He probably threw it in the bathroom trash, so it's still there. We find it, stick it back on his butt, and give him a couple of shots of tequila. We'll make sure he scrubs down, and we'll wrap him up in something, like a shower curtain, and take him out to Montauk. We can roll him out somewhere in the dunes. He won't wake up for a day, so that will give us plenty of time to pack up and drive home. What do you think?"

Deb reached for a bottle of wine and her red plastic cup. "The patch is for seventy-two hours. It might still be effective. That might work."

Kelly was frowning. "Scrub down?"

"We can't risk DNA or fibers," I said. "Don't you watch *CSI*?"

"We're really going to leave him naked on a beach somewhere?" Kelly asked. "That seems a bit harsh."

Deb waved one hand. "No, that's not harsh. That's just the sort of thing that will put this over the top. Jason will probably tell everyone he was used as a sex slave. He'll be in *US Weekly* for a whole month." Deb drained her little red cup. "Thank God we have a plan," she said, struggling to open another bottle. "Where's the pie?"

We made ourselves comfortable in the sand, cutting and eating cherry pie and drinking more wine.

"We might," Kelly said, "be able to just come back here and, you know, hang. The FBI has already been here, right?"

I felt a grin. "True. With Jason gone, we don't *have* to leave."

Deb nudged me. "Giving you a few extra days with Andy?"

"Well, that too." I drank my wine. "It would be nice to spend time with him without worrying he'll have to read me my rights."

"I'm worried," Kelly said slowly, "about Jason. What his story will be. You know he's not too good about thinking on his feet."

"He's not great at thinking, period," Deb muttered. "But what choice do we have? We could cut out his tongue, but he could always be taught to write."

"He can always say he can't remember. He's been drugged. That would be fairly believable," I said.

"I say it's worth a risk," Deb said. "Tonight?"

We all nodded and stretched back in the sun. We had about an hour of good warmth left. I was daydreaming about Andy again. It was kind of explicit, actually, when we were interrupted. A dog was barking. A familiar bark.

"Did he let that damn dog out?" Deb groused.

I propped myself up on one elbow and shaded my eyes with my hands.

I blinked.

No, I was not hallucinating.

Muffy was wiggling her way down the beach, yapping.

And behind her, tottering on her usual stilettos, was Tina.

"I felt so bad about leaving you," Tina said. "Really. I'm so sorry. I took a cab back here, all the way from Hoboken. It cost me a fortune. But this is all my fault." She dropped to her knees in the sand. She was wearing, of course, perfectly inappropriate beachwear: skintight black capris, a purple sequined halter, and a black-leather moto jacket. "Tell me what I can do."

I stared, first at her, then at Deb. Deb's eyes were narrow. I knew she was furious.

"You can turn around and go right back to where you came from," Deb said. "Only this time, take that mangy dog with you."

Tina looked crushed. "I said I was sorry," she wailed. "I'm here to make things right!"

"Oh, good Lord," Kelly muttered beside me.

"Does Jason know you're back?" Deb asked.

Tina looked a bit uncomfortable. "Yes. And I must say he did not seem too happy. But I had to check on him to make sure he was okay! What have you all been doing to him?"

"This is not good," Deb said to me. I just shook my head.

Oh, Tina, why?

"We need to get off the beach," I said. "Tina, why didn't you dye your hair back to anything but purple?"

We gathered our towels, wine bottles, and leftovers and then trooped back to the house. Jason was obviously in his room, I imagined, with the door locked. Possibly bolted. Tina was silent. I almost felt sorry for her. Her heart was probably in the right place, but, as usual, her brain was nowhere to be found.

"Annie?" she whimpered. "What did I do this time?"

"First, answer me this. Why did you leave?"

She looked uncomfortable. "Well, it was like, he didn't really want to have, you know, sex. With me." She rolled her eyes heavenward, as though seeking a divine explanation. "Even after I flat-out suggested it. I mean, what kind of man says no to somebody like me?"

Several answers came to mind, but I kept my mouth shut.

"And then . . ."

Did I really want to hear this?

"Then in the morning, he just rolled over and said no. He wanted to sleep instead. *Sleep.*"

She wrestled Muffy closer to her chest. "I was just so . . . hurt. I couldn't imagine facing him. But when I got home, I realized that the situation with Jason was bigger than me and my feelings. So here I am. And I don't understand why you are all so upset."

Oh, dear. If only I'd made a list. "Tina, here's the thing. We're in real trouble now. We tried to do something to get Jason out of here, and it backfired. In a very big way. So we're really desperate right now, and we think we have a plan. Your being here is just . . . an added complication."

"But see, I can help you fix things," she said, brightening. "Just tell me what to do."

I left her in the living room and helped in the kitchen. We spent ten minutes cleaning up in silence. Well, not really. We spent ten minutes cleaning up while listening to the news. The lead story was about the extended search for two women, possibly a couple, one of them an actress, who, in addition to kidnapping Jason Wilde, sent a kindly little old man to the hospital by threatening him with a gun.

Tina stood in front of the television, transfixed. "Are they talking about you?" she finally asked. "What did you do?"

We told her about the confrontation with Artie. "It seemed," Kelly said, "to be a good idea at the time."

Deb knocked on Jason's door. He came shuffling out into the living room and sat on the couch. Muffy immediately abandoned her mistress to jump on his lap, wriggling with pure happiness, her butt and tail shaking like crazy.

He sniffed and looked at us with a decidedly uncooperative glare. "What?"

I sat down next to him. "Jason, here's the thing. We really need to get you out of here. We have a plan, and we're pretty sure it will work, but we need to make sure your story will be straight."

"My story?"

"Yes." Deb's voice was calm and patient. She was a nurse. She probably used the same voice on the old, crazy people who wandered into the ER. "The best thing for you to tell police is that you were drugged most of the time and you don't remember anything. Do you think you can stick to that?"

"Drugged? And don't remember? Ah, come on, I need more than that. After all, everyone is going to want a piece of this. I have to tell them *something*." Jason frowned. That usually meant he was hard at work, thinking. "Maybe some torture? Or maybe, you know"—he dropped his voice—"sex stuff?"

Deb sighed. "Told you," she said, to the room at large.

I made a rude noise. Kelly just shook her head and grinned at me.

"What?" Jason asked. "It could happen!"

"Jason, it's just that you'll have to keep so much stuff straight in your mind. And you'll be examined, I'm sure, by a doctor, and, well, there won't be any, ah, physical evidence to back up a story like that," I told him.

"Unless," Tina piped up, "you want us to . . . well, hurt you."

Jason narrowed his eyes at her. "No. Maybe simple is best."

"Here's what we need you to do," I said. "Take a long, hot shower. We'll give you a towel to wear. Does anyone remember what we did with that patch?"

He shrugged. "It's still sitting on the end table."

I went into his room and there it was, crumpled by the lamp. I brought it out to Deb.

"See, there's still some gel," she said. "That means there's medication left. We can use this again. We'll get you into the car. You can have a few drinks. Once you pass out, we'll drive you to a deserted stretch of beach and leave you there to be found."

He did not look happy. "All night?"

She nodded.

"Am I going to be, like, naked?"

Deb nodded again. "We can't afford to have anything lead back to us. You do understand, right?"

He shrugged. "Yeah, I guess, but what if nobody finds me? I could get sick being out in the cold all night. And then get all sunburned and shit."

Kelly cleared her throat. "Good point. We'll make an anonymous call to the FBI."

"And I'll be passed out?" Jason asked.

Deb nodded. "That way, it will look more believable when you tell the police you were drugged the whole time."

He didn't look happy. "Why can't we all go to the beach, and then I can put on the patch and have a few drinks with all of you?"

"Because," I said, "there's a chance someone might be wandering around the beach and see us together."

He frowned. "I didn't think of that. Well, how about you drop me off, and I do the whole patch-and-tequila thing by myself?"

Deb sighed patiently. "Jason, do you really think you could sit there, waiting by yourself, naked on the beach?"

He shook his head. "Probably not. What about my clothes?"

"I'll take them home, wash them, and donate them to Goodwill," I told him.

He nodded. "And my phone? I got a lotta important stuff on my phone."

"Don't you think," I said, "it would look odd if you're naked but have your phone?"

Jason shrugged. "Yeah. I guess." He looked around. "When?"

"Tonight," Kelly said.

"What?" Tina squeaked. "But I just got back!"

Deb looked over her glasses. The Look of Death. "Just in time to spend a few more carefree days with your friends, right?"

Tina's shoulders slumped. "Right."

"Exactly," I said. "Okay, Jason, we'll leave around midnight. Right before we leave, you'll shower and stick on your patch. Have a few drinks in the car on the ride over, and we'll roll you out. Then we stop at a pay phone, call the Feds, and make our way back here." I glanced around. "Sound good, everyone?"

Kelly raised a tentative hand. "I haven't seen a pay phone in about three years."

We were all silent. Good point.

"Surely, there's a pay phone *somewhere*?" Deb said. "Even in the Hamptons, there has to be at least one cell-phone-hating whack job who occasionally needs to make a call."

"I'm sure," I said. "But we don't want to spend the rest of the night driving around looking for one while Jason is freezing his assets off on the beach."

Kelly was on her phone. She did not look happy. "I can't find a site that tells you where pay phones are," she said. "Can you believe it?"

"Maybe you all should drive out there now," Tina suggested. "You know, kind of scout out the pay-phone situation. I can stay here and keep Jason company."

"No," said Deb sharply. "You are not going to be keeping Jason company. We need . . ." She looked at Kelly. "Liam would probably know. He seems the type who probably needs to use an untraceable phone all the time."

Kelly nodded and pressed a button. "Liam? It's me. Listen, do you happen to know if there's a pay phone anywhere out in Montauk? It can't be *in* someplace. It has to be just, like, you know, hanging out on the street." She made a face and took a deep breath. "Of course it has to do with Jason." She frowned. "No, you don't need to know anything else. Please, just tell me." She got off the couch and began to pace. "Liam, please don't make me drive out there and hurt you," she said, channeling her inner dominatrix and sounding positively threatening. "Because, believe me, I will." She listened for a bit longer. "Good. That's great, thanks. Now, can you think of a place out there that's not open yet for the season? You know, someplace that would be . . . quiet?" She smiled. "Thanks, Liam. I owe you, but don't expect too much, okay?" She hung up the phone and grabbed a napkin and started scribbling. "Got it," she told us. "We have a motel out there, on the beach, that's not opened yet. And the pay phone is a mile away, next to the bus stop on Euclid. We're solid." She looked around.

Deb clapped her hands together. "Okay, ladies. Looks like this is a go."

Everyone looked relieved. Except, of course, Tina.

It was a quiet evening. We snacked and sipped wine. We listened to the news, of course. No further word of Artie. No further mention of $5 million. Apparently, the FBI was no longer issuing any statements. A representative of Jason's television show, when asked about where the ransom money was coming from, refused to answer.

Things were getting tense.

Andy and I texted back and forth. He was vague about what he was doing, but wondered if I could get away.

"Call Andy," Kelly said, after watching me for about twenty minutes. "It's obvious you want to see him again. Go."

I got off the couch and went outside on the deck.

He answered on the fourth ring. "You look pretty good on television," I told him.

He chuckled. "Oh, yeah. I bet."

"I had no idea you were such a big shot. Hanging out at press conferences and all."

"Technically, this is my turf. Suffolk and Nassau Counties fall under the jurisdiction of the Long Island Resident Agency, which is mine. But it's a celebrity, so of course the big guns from New York City rolled in. It's best to just smile and nod. Are you doing anything tonight?"

I felt a tingle that started in my stomach and spread out in all sorts of interesting directions. Actually, I was getting ready to escort a well-known kidnapping victim out to a deserted beach where I would help roll him, naked, onto the sand. "Had a quick dinner, hanging with the girls. You? Any big interviews scheduled?"

"No, thank God. I can maybe get out in about an hour. A drink somewhere? John Scott's?"

"A deal. I'll see you then."

I went back into the house.

"I'm meeting Andy down the street," I said, trying to keep the excitement out of my voice. Jason made a funny noise, and Kelly threw a pillow at him.

"Be home by midnight. Have a great time," Deb said. "See if he can talk about the case. You know, maybe get a clue as to what they're looking at."

"I am not," I said, "going to pump him for information."

"Of course not," Kelly soothed. "But it would be natural for you to ask."

She was right. I shrugged and went upstairs and changed clothes. I had nothing that would be considered vaguely date-worthy, but then I reminded myself it was John Scott's. I pulled on dark jeans and Deb's tunic that I'd worn to the American. Had that really been only three days ago?

I looked long and hard in the bathroom mirror. I had never been a vain person. I had always been generally unconcerned with the way I looked, you know? At that moment, I have to admit, I was hoping for a minor miracle. But, no, there was nothing to be done there. My hair was not going to magically straighten itself out, my puffy jawline was not going to melt away, and my eyelashes were not going to magically reappear. I tried a bit of mascara, and not even that worked. I put some lipstick on and gratefully remembered how badly lit John Scott's was at night.

I turned, walked out of the bathroom, and straight into Jason.

"Don't you knock?" I asked.

"The door was open," he pointed out.

"Oh. Well. What do you want?"

"I want to make sure you don't blow things with this Andy guy," Jason said.

I narrowed my eyes at him. "What do you mean?"

He shrugged. "You don't take lots of chances, Annie. But you should. You are one remarkable woman. I've watched you. I know how smart you are. You're able to look around and find the best solution. But you're so afraid to act. Why is that?"

I stared at him, my throat closing with sudden tears. How could he do that?

"I have no idea what you're talking about," I bluffed.

He shook his head sadly. "Yes, you do. You have a path in front of you. It's neat and pretty to look at, and you know what to expect. You can look all around you and see what's going on, and maybe you're even excited by all of it. But you're afraid to step off your path, Annie. Don't be. Sure, it can be scary, but that's what makes it so much fun."

"I'm a little too old," I said, fighting to keep my voice even, "for fun." How could he put into words what I'd been unable to admit, even to myself?

He shook his head. "You're never too old. In fact, it's what keeps you young. It sounds like you're really interested in this guy. And don't look at me and tell me you're not thinking about passion either. Take the step. Even if it's messy. Even if it scares you. Especially if it scares you. Just close your eyes and go."

"I don't even know him."

"Sure you do. You know everything about Andy that you need to know. Stop making excuses for staying where you are. You have so much ahead of you if you just let it happen."

I closed my eyes very tightly. When I opened them, he was still standing there.

"Okay?"

"Okay. But tell me this, Jason. For a guy who's been stumbling around like an idiot for days, how did you get to be so smart all of a sudden?"

He looked at the floor and shrugged. "I don't know lots of stuff," he said. "But I know people."

"Yes. You do. Jason, can I ask you something?"

He nodded. "Sure. Anything."

"How did you get here?"

He frowned. "I met you guys at the American Hotel, remember? And I passed out and—"

"No. I know how you got *here*, to Dune Road. I meant, how did you end up going along with this crazy scheme of Artie's in the first place."

He shrugged again and pushed his hands deep into the front pockets of his jeans. "I wanted to be an actor for as long as I can remember," he said. "I wanted to make people happy. I just wasn't very good at it. But Artie believed in me. He did everything he could for me. He got the first series, and then all those movies. They were awful, I know, but I kept working. And now this show is just, well . . ."

He blew out through his mouth. "They don't want to renew my contract. I know that. If I don't have this show, I can't imagine what I'll do with my life. I know that's what is behind all this. Artie knows that this will make it harder for the producer to just throw me away. So I have to trust Artie. He always tried his best for me. I'm not so good at working things out for myself, you know?"

I leaned forward to kiss him on the cheek, turned, and then went downstairs and into the night.

It had stayed warm—maybe sixty degrees—and the skies were clear. It was a beautiful night, and as I came into the parking lot, I could see Andy sitting by the window. I forced myself to keep from running the last few steps.

The bar was almost empty, barely a half-dozen tables occupied. I slid into the chair across from Andy.

"Hey."

His smile almost broke my heart. "Hey, yourself. Beer? Wine? Are you hungry?"

"Wine," I said, and watched him as he went up to the bar. He had changed out of his suit and was back in those well-fitting jeans. Under a denim jacket he was wearing a white button-down shirt open at the collar, showing just a bit of dark chest hair. As he sat back down across from me, I kept my eyes on that tiny patch of fuzz and kept wondering how it would feel if I pressed my palm against it.

"So, what did you do today?" he asked.

Hmm . . . let's see. Today I followed Kelly into a miserable dive bar and watched as she put on a performance worthy of Masterpiece *Theatre*, even though the final act resulted in a little old man being taken to the hospital. Oh, and I was now officially identified as the possibly lesbian kidnapper.

"Got a visit from a few of your coworkers. You?"

He sighed. "Yeah, doing the old house-to-house. With all of our technology, most of what we do is still old-fashioned grunt work." He shook his head. "This case is . . . off. There's something wrong, and I can't put my finger on it." His hand was on the table, palm-side down. He tapped his index finger a few times. "Something is wrong."

His fingers were long and beautifully shaped, dark hair on his knuckles, the nails smooth and buffed.

Take a step. Take a step.

I moved my own hand over his, and as I did, he turned his, palm-side up, and the feel of his skin against mine sent the blood rushing to my head so fast I could barely breathe.

"Oh?"

He curled his middle finger, just a bit, and it brushed against my palm. By now, I was feeling . . . itchy.

"Yeah. This whole case is a bitch."

I was watching our hands. I pressed my fingers down, against his palm, and then I looked up into his eyes. They were so dark and full of longing I almost cried.

I thought about my flabby thighs. I had passed on the bikini wax. Joe always laughed at me because he said I made funny noises when we made love. Messy.

Then I thought about what Jason had said.

"Can you talk about it? The case, I mean?" What was I saying? Of course he couldn't talk about it. And the blood was pounding in my ears so loud, even if he spilled top-secret info, I wouldn't be able to hear it properly.

"The ransom note doesn't make sense."

I slipped my foot out of my shoe and found his ankle under the table. I slid my toes under the cuff of his jeans and leaned forward.

"Really?"

His mouth twitched. I swallowed hard. Talk about stepping off the path. Trying to convey a come-hither sensibility with your foot was probably about as off the path as you could get.

"Yeah. I mean, who slips a ransom note under the front door and then sends a photocopy to the show's producer? Those two women, meeting Sherman in the open like that? Who does that? It's like everyone is playing the kidnapping game, but nobody knows their lines."

My toes were sliding up the back of his calf. From where I was sitting, he had great legs.

"Doesn't make sense," I said, somewhat breathlessly. His fingertips were gently stroking my wrist, which meant he could feel my quickened heartbeat.

"Nothing about this makes sense," he said, and I knew he wasn't talking about Jason anymore.

"I don't usually do this," I told him, sliding my foot farther up and tickling the back of his knee. His palm was hot and dry, and by now I think there were actual sparks jumping out from where our skin was touching.

"Do what? Use your toes as a method of seduction?"

"Seduce at all. In fact, after my divorce, I pretty much figured my sex life was over."

He lifted my hand and brought it to his lips. "It doesn't have to be," he said, and kissed my palm.

My foot had pretty much gone as far as it could go. I slid it back to the floor and into my shoe.

Okay. Jason said to close my eyes and jump. I was ready. But I did have standards.

"I'm too old for bathroom sex in a bar," I said.

"Me too. How about the backseat of my car?"

"How big is it?"

"Honda Civic."

"Crap. That won't work."

"Maybe we could just walk this off," he said.

"You mean, like, on the beach?"

"Yeah." His breathing was getting rough.

I pulled my hand away, gulped my wine, and stood up. "Let's go."

We walked out into the parking lot. As soon as we were out of the pool of light from the front door, he pulled me to him and kissed me. But it was more than a kiss. His hands were under my sweater, and I was tugging at his shirt, trying to get my hands on his skin. He was so tall, and at one point he reached down and picked me up off the ground, and I wrapped my legs around his hips.

"I'm also too old for parking-lot sex," I finally gasped.

He loosened his arms, and I slid back to the ground. He grabbed my hand, and we practically ran across Dune Road.

I knew the territory. We went through the parking lot of the wall of condos, skirted the empty pool, then broke out onto the deserted beach. I turned right, away from number 461.

The moon was half-full. It was just bright enough for us to find a break in the dune grass in front of a huge dark-shingled home.

We kissed some more. It was hard keeping our mouths together while tearing our clothes off, so we broke apart.

I felt a moment of panic. "What if somebody sees us?" I asked, kicking my shoes away.

"The owners aren't here," Andy said, pulling off his shirt.

"How do you know?" I asked, wrestling with the zipper of my jeans.

"We checked every house along the beach, remember?"

He pulled the sweater up and over my head. His hands went around my back, snapped open my bra, then moved down to my butt.

By the time I hit the sand, I'd pretty much forgotten where the stupid house even was.

Chapter Ten

I'd only been with one man in my whole life. Joe. After the divorce, I had fervently hoped that I would once again have a sex life, so I had carefully planned out my next sexual excursion. It involved candles and a little Marvin Gaye playing in the background. It did not involve sand, moonlight, and the pounding of waves, which was a mistake on my part, because—wow.

My brain was terrified of crabs and nocturnal, flesh-craving seagulls, or the distinct possibility that someone with a flashlight would find us, or even hear us. But I stopped thinking as my body responded to his lips against my neck, and the feathering of his fingertips on my skin. His body was long and lean, hard muscle beneath rough skin, and he was hot. Not *Ooh, look, he's hot* hot, but there was heat coming off him that made me forget all about the cool, damp sand and the breeze off the ocean. It was too dark to see much, so I explored with my hands. The flat muscles of his chest eased into narrow hips. His shoulders were broad and muscled. There was a long, knotty scar down his left leg.

We talked to each other—like more familiar lovers do. The sound of the surf was loud, but I could still hear him moan softly, and his hands in my hair were gentle.

When was the last time I'd felt like this? I threw my head back and gasped, waiting for actual fireworks to burst in the night sky. As I slid back onto the sand, I kept breathing in lungfuls of air as I tried to calm the rushing of my blood and steady the world around me. I felt myself grinning in the darkness as my entire body slowly went from *Oh, my God* to *Ah . . . indeed.*

I wouldn't have cared if an entire flock of birds had settled around us, each with a spotlight and microphone.

I rolled against him, and his arms went around me. I could feel the beating of his heart, and his lips were in my hair. I could have fallen asleep right there, on a dark beach with a man I'd known less than a week. I had never felt so safe.

"I don't suppose we can stay here forever?" I finally asked.

He laughed softly. "Probably not. Do you need help with your clothes?"

Getting dressed by moonlight is not nearly as exciting as getting naked in the moonlight, but we managed. Afterward, we sat by the edge of the water, talking. His arm was around my shoulder, and even though the temperature had dropped, I felt warm and almost content. I had managed to forget, for a little while, that this man could be the person to ruin my life by arresting me and putting me behind bars for several years. I tried to avoid thinking about the whole Jason situation for as long as I could.

"Promise you won't freak out if I tell you something?" I asked him.

"Promise."

"You're only the second man I've ever done that with."

He drew back and stared. "What? Made love on the beach?"

"No. Made love, period. I met my ex, Joe, in high school. He was my first and only. Until you."

He looked thoughtfully into the dark. "Well, I suppose I should be grateful that, if nothing else, I'm at least the second-best lover you've ever had."

I laughed and laid my head on his shoulder. "You're the *very* best lover I've ever had in a sand dune, at night, in May."

"Well, there you go. Do I get a ribbon? Cupcake?"

I stretched up to kiss his cheek. "I think a trophy. I'll have one engraved."

"Now that will certainly give the jeweler something to talk about."

We were silent for a few moments.

"How did you become an FBI agent?"

He shrugged. "I applied while I was still in law school. I loved the law, but I didn't think being a lawyer was going to make me happy. I spent my entire childhood playing cops and robbers, so I thought I might try making a living chasing bad guys."

"Do you catch many of them?"

He nodded. "Yep. I love the chase, you know? Seeing how everything fits together, finding the pattern. That's why this Wilde thing is making me crazy. There's no pattern. It's all just a bunch of random clues thrown together that don't make sense. Something else is going on here. I just have to figure out what it is."

I almost told him then. It would have been such a relief. I knew that he might very well have handcuffed me without a second thought. I also knew there was a good chance I'd never see him again, except perhaps in court. And I think if it had been just about me, I would have. But I couldn't make a decision for my friends.

I also didn't want to pump him for any information, but—

"So, do you have any suspects?"

He shook his head. "Everybody. We're trying to find out who he was in the American Hotel with. A blonde, a brunette, and a skinny, younger girl with purple hair. The bartender said they weren't regulars. So, basically, any three women in New York. There are a lot more women with purple hair than you'd think. It's a mess."

I realized how lucky we were. If Roy had been tending bar, we would have been a lot closer to being picked up. As it was, I kept thanking God that Deb not joining us that night was throwing Andy off our scent.

We talked about breakfast the next morning. Maybe, I said. I knew that early tomorrow he would be retrieving Jason's naked and drugged body off a stretch of Montauk beach.

He kissed me. Then we talked some more. I finally insisted I had to leave, and he walked me down the beach. He turned to go back to John Scott's. I continued down, hoping I'd be able to find 461 in the dark.

I should not have worried. I easily recognized it because all the lights were still on.

I came in through the sliding glass doors. Everyone was, of course, watching the news. "Sorry, I lost track of time. Are we getting ready to go?"

Deb looked at me from over the top of her glasses. "It's just now eleven. We have time. The real question is, how, exactly, did you lose track of time?"

"We were on the beach. Talking."

Deb lifted her eyebrow. "And how, exactly, did your sweater end up being inside out?"

I looked down at myself. Crap.

"High passion," Jason quipped. "I hope you took my advice."

"Listen, guys, Andy talked a little about the case," I said, crossing over to the kitchen. It's not that I wanted to change the subject, although I really *did* want to change the subject, but what Andy had said was important.

"I told you," Jason said with a smirk. "Gets them talking every time."

Kelly followed me to the kitchen. "What did he say?"

"He says it's a mess. They can't make any sense of it," I told them. "The ransom note is off, the whole thing with Artie—the whole thing is off." I shook my head. "Jason, I really hope this works."

He nodded glumly. "Me too. Listen, I—" He stopped, then took a deep breath. "I never meant to put anyone in a position like this. It was all supposed to be, well, a prank. Artie kept telling me nobody was going to get in trouble, and he'd always been right before. I think that maybe, this time, he was afraid. He let Leo call the shots. That was a mistake, and I should have realized it." He moved his shoulders around. "I'm really sorry."

Deb crossed over and actually gave him a hug. "It's going to be okay. Now, go take a shower and give us all your clothes."

Jason emerged, some minutes later, wrapped in a hot-pink beach towel and nothing else. His hair was slicked back, his stubble glistened with droplets, and his skin was smooth and absolutely touchable.

I could not wait to have him gone.

We got into the car and drove east. Jason stuck the Fentanyl patch back on as we left the house. He sat between Tina and me in the back of the Prius, still wrapped in his towel, drinking tequila from a water bottle.

"So tell me, really," he said, "are you all going to miss me?"

"Like a toothache," Deb growled from the front seat. "Or maybe constipation."

"Ah, Deb, my girl," Jason laughed. "Was it really that bad?"

Tina leaned toward him. "I'll miss you, Jason. Terribly. But I'll find a way to get in touch with you after, you know, all of this has blown over."

Jason took another long pull on the tequila. "Tina, no offense, but please don't." His voice was starting to slur. "I mean that. Don't. Ever."

Deb was driving carefully. I saw her constantly looking in her rearview mirror. "Jason, what are you going to tell the FBI?" she asked.

He was leaning back against the seat. "Drugged. The whole time. Don't remember . . ."

He was out like a light by the time we hit Bridgehampton.

In Montauk, we found the pay phone first, where Liam said it would be—by the bus stop. And there, a bit farther down the road, was the police station. Deb pulled over to the side of the road. Tina started whimpering.

"If we call the police from here, they'll find him in, like, five minutes," I said. "How would we make our escape? We probably wouldn't even make it to the highway."

Deb tapped the steering wheel with her fingertips. "You're right. This is not good. At all. We need to be much farther away."

"Well, if there's a phone at this bus stop, maybe there's one at another," I said. "Or at a jitney stop? Kelly? We need another pay phone. Find us the farthest bus stop or jitney stop from Montauk."

She squinted in the darkness and began tapping on her phone.

Jason began snoring softly. Tina started to put her hand to his head.

"Don't touch him," I snapped. "Just our luck you'll lose a fingernail in there, and the police will trace your nail gel right back to us."

"I've found another jitney stop. Over by that little airport," Kelly said. "Is that far enough away?"

"Yep," I told her. "Let's find this hotel or whatever. Liam said it was closed?"

Deb nodded as she turned the car around. "I saw it coming in. It's right down the road here. It's not supposed to open until July."

It was a dark and shuttered little place, looking sad in the moonlight. We drove past the tiny cabins and pulled up fairly close to the water. As Tina and I tried to get Jason out of the backseat, the towel was pulled off, and we dragged him naked onto the sand. Deb, swearing furiously, got the towel, then spread it out neatly on the ground beside him.

"We'll roll him over on the towel, then use it to drag him," Kelly said. "The less we touch him the better."

Deb and I pushed him gently over onto his stomach, using our feet, and we each grabbed a corner of the towel and pulled.

It wasn't nearly as hard as getting him up our staircase on Dune Road, but in the darkness we had a problem staying on the path. When we finally made it out to the beach, we were all breathing a little heavy, and not just from staring at his beautiful butt reflecting in the pale moonlight.

"Where should we leave him?" I asked.

Kelly looked around. "Why not right here? We don't want the FBI to have to search for him. We want him easily found."

We rolled him again, this time onto the sand. I felt kind of bad. It was windy out, and I knew the sand would be cold and damp.

"Do we have to take the towel?" I asked. "He might catch cold."

Deb was folding the towel, muttering under her breath. "He'll be fine. Let's just get out of here."

We trooped back to the car and swung back onto Route 27.

"Should we go back and erase our tire tracks?" Kelly asked.

"Oh, God, really?" I said. "I would think all they could do is say, 'Yep, a Prius.'"

"Let's hope," Tina muttered.

"I am so glad this is over," Deb said. "I swear I've aged at least ten years."

Kelly laughed shakily. "I don't know. It was kind of exciting, being wanted by the police."

"We still are," I reminded her. "In fact, we'll probably be on their most-wanted list forever. After all, we are possibly armed and dangerous."

Deb started laughing too. "Yes, we're desperadoes. Something else to scratch off my bucket list."

"I can't believe I missed it," Tina whined.

I patted her arm. "Tina, believe me, you really didn't miss all that much."

We drove through Westhampton Beach and on to MacArthur airport. Kelly directed us to a lone pay phone by the jitney stop. We had the number to the hotline that had been established by the local police. I jumped out of the car, made the call, and was back in the car in less than a minute. We headed back to Dune Road.

We'd done it. Sometime in the next hour, Jason would be in a hospital bed. All we had to do was spend the next two days laying low and enjoying what was left of our vacation.

It was after four in the morning before we got to bed. We tried to stay awake and watch the news, to hear if something had broken in the case of kidnapped Jason Wilde, but it looked like the authorities were taking their sweet time getting out to Montauk. So I was fairly comatose when Andy called me, just before seven, to ask if I still wanted to meet him for breakfast.

"You sound groggy," I told him. "Have you been up all night?"

He sighed heavily over the phone. "Yeah. We got a tip that there was some guy on a beach in Montauk, but it turned out to be a wild-goose chase."

I shot up in bed. "Oh, my."

"Yeah. Here is something else that's wrong with this case. Whoever called was very specific. Those kinds of callers we pay special attention to. And when we got there, it looked like maybe there had been someone out there, but whoever it was, was gone. So, you hungry?"

What? He was gone? Jason was *gone*? "Actually, Andy, this morning is kind of booked. Really booked. I mean, *tons* of stuff to do. Can I call you after lunch?"

He chuckled. "This isn't a bad-performance kiss-off, is it?"

In spite of my soaring anxiety, I felt myself start to blush. "Ah, no. Not at all. Like I told you, there may be a trophy involved. I'll call. I promise."

I clicked off the phone and stared out the window. Jason was gone. Jason was gone.

Where?

Suddenly, I couldn't breathe. I tried to yell, but there was nothing. I climbed out of bed and ran into Kelly's room.

She woke immediately. "What? Annie, calm down."

I sat on the edge of her bed, dropping my head down between my knees and taking deep, cleansing breaths. I finally felt my pulse start to slow down.

"It's Jason. They didn't find him."

"What do you mean, they didn't find him?"

I looked at her. "Andy just called. He was out all night. He went to Montauk. But they didn't find Jason."

Kelly turned white.

"But you called them," she said. "You told them exactly where he was."

I nodded. "Yes, and they got the call. But when they went out there, he was gone. Andy said that they could tell somebody had been there, but . . . Jason was gone."

Deb was awake in bed, watching the news, and frowning as we burst into her room.

"How come there's nothing on about Jason?" she demanded.

"Because he wasn't found," I told her. "He was gone when the FBI got there. I just got off the phone with Andy. Could he have woken up?"

Deb shook her head. "No. He was good for at least ten hours of la-la land."

Kelly's hand flew to her mouth. "Oh, no. Did he drown? Was he too close to the water?"

Deb got out of bed and was staring at the carpet. "No, he didn't drown."

"Well, where did he go?" I asked, my voice a little high-pitched and wild. "Why didn't they find him?"

Deb closed her eyes and shook her head. "Somebody else found him first," she said.

"But why would anyone want to take Jason?" Kelly asked.

"Because," Deb said, "the entire world thinks that, somewhere out there, five million dollars is being wrapped up and getting ready to be dropped off."

Five million dollars. I'd forgotten about that.

"So, somebody followed us, and after we dragged him down on the beach and made sure he was safe and dry and then called the FBI so that he would be found, they came along and *stole* him?" I asked. I stared at her. "No one knew where he was but us. Unless some random midnight beach walker stumbled on him and figured, hey, let's take this guy home."

Kelly's eyes filled with tears. "Oh, no, poor Jason!" she cried. "This is so bad."

I felt something in the pit of my stomach. It was more than anger. Somewhere, there was a little spark of vengeance. And can I tell you?

I'm really not a revenge type of person, so I was a bit surprised by my reaction. "Whoever did this had better not hurt him, that's all I've got to say. Because if someone does, I will hunt him down."

Kelly sniffed as she spoke. "I thought you said he was a selfish jerk. Thoughtless and irresponsible."

"Maybe he is, or maybe he isn't," I said. "But he's ours." I took a deep breath. "We've got to steal him back."

It was not a cheerful breakfast. In fact, we were all downright grim. Even Kelly could find nothing positive to say, and when that happened, you knew things were bad.

"First, we need to figure out who took him," Deb said, shredding her pancakes with her fork and knife.

Kelly cleared her throat. "Let's face it. It was Liam."

I glanced up at her. "We don't know that," I said.

"Yes, we do. He was the only one who knew we had Jason in the first place. We don't know anything about him, except that's he's probably a shady character. And remember, somewhere, five million dollars is involved. That's a whole lot of money." Her jaw was set. She was getting tough.

Deb sighed. "You're sure?"

"I'll call him right now," she said. "Ask him to come over. We'll get it out of him."

"How?" Deb asked. "We have nothing to hold over him. How can we force him to tell us anything? He'll probably just laugh at us. We've got nothing."

"But we do," Kelly said. "He might not really be in the Witness Protection Program, but there's something going on. He wants to stay under the radar. We can threaten him with . . . something."

"Facebook," Tina said. "We can post pictures of him on Facebook. Or a YouTube video. We can make him go viral."

I nodded. "Great idea. Kelly, call him."

Kelly took a deep breath and took out her cell phone. "Liam? Yes, it's me. Listen, do you think you could stop by the house? Like, now?"

She listened. "No, it won't take very long. It's kind of, well, a favor."

She listened, then lowered her voice. "No, really. Please?" She clicked off the phone. "He's coming."

Deb reached over and shook her shoulder. "Good job, Kelly."

We cleaned up, then sat around in a quiet circle at the table, waiting. I felt terrible. Not only was our problem *not* solved, but now it was worse because Jason was with someone else. Someone who wanted $5 million. Someone who didn't necessarily have Jason's best interest at heart.

I felt afraid for him. I felt afraid for us. I wanted to grab Kelly's hand and sing "Kumbaya."

It didn't take Liam long. Kelly let him in without a word. He looked at us, smiling.

"And who might you be, darlin'?" he asked Tina.

"Your worst nightmare," she shot back.

His smile quickly faded. "Why," he asked, "do I feel like I'm about to take a hit?"

Kelly cleared her throat as she sat down beside him. "All we want," she said, "is to get Jason back."

Liam frowned. "From where?"

Deb drummed her fingers against the table. "From wherever you stashed him."

He looked indignant. "Are you suggesting I have Jason? I thought he'd be at the intersection of a pay phone and a deserted motel."

"He should have been," Kelly said. "But he's not. We left him to be found by the FBI, but someone else found him first. And took him."

Liam looked at her. "And you think *I* did it?"

Kelly stayed tough. "No one else knew, Liam."

He grabbed her hand. "Kelly, darlin', I swear on my mother's grave, I was nowhere near Montauk last night."

Tina's phone flashed and clicked. "I'm going to post this on Facebook," she said. "In three minutes. I'm going to send it out to all my followers and ask them to share. With any luck, your picture, and the address of the vineyard, will be spread all over the Internet in a few hours.

Liam turned white. "You can't do that."

Deb clasped her hands together, rings clicking. "Yes, Liam. We can and we will. Unless you tell us where Jason is."

He shook his head frantically. "I don't know. I do not know." He turned to Kelly again. "Please believe me. Why would I do such a thing?"

"For five million dollars?" Kelly suggested.

He shook his head. "Listen, ladies, I'm not saying I'm above working outside the box for some quick cash, but would I really want to risk being caught? And have my face and name all over the national press? No amount of money is worth that."

I glanced around. Deb's lips twisted. She sat back, frowning.

"We hadn't thought about that," Kelly said slowly.

Liam held her hand tightly in both of his. "Kelly. Believe me. I've built a good life here. I wouldn't want to ruin it. It's not like I can just pick up and go if things here get dicey."

Kelly stared at their hands. "If it wasn't you, who else could it possibly be?"

"Artie," I said. "Artie knew where Jason was. And Leo."

"But Artie was in the hospital," Kelly said. "Besides, I got the impression that Artie didn't really want to go along with the kidnapping idea. He said that Leo was the brains of the outfit."

"But what do we know about Leo?" I was staring off in the general direction of Liam, who was looking less nervous. "I bet Leo is a real creep."

"Who's Leo?" Liam asked.

Kelly shushed him and looked thoughtful.

"But how would Leo even know where we were?" Deb asked. "Artie didn't know, so how could Leo?"

I was thinking hard. "But that's the thing. Artie did know," I said. "Artie said he tracked Jason through his phone. And the phone didn't die right away, remember? It was working for the first day or two. So Artie knew where Jason was all along, and he must have told Leo."

"There was a car parked across the street from our drive when the taxi dropped me off yesterday," Tina said suddenly. "It was just sitting in the driveway, and there was someone in it. I noticed because the house seemed to be closed up."

"What kind of car?" Deb asked.

Tina wrinkled her brow. "A white Cadillac."

Kelly looked horrified. "You mean Leo was casing the joint? Like, a real criminal?"

"Kelly, hon," Deb said, "I'm pretty sure that Leo is a real criminal. After all, if he did grab Jason, I bet it isn't to keep him safe for the police."

"Why didn't we notice it?" Kelly asked.

"Because from the street, you can see us coming down the drive," I said. "Whoever was there had plenty of time to ease out and into the street and drive off."

"And then follow us?" Kelly asked.

I nodded, feeling excited. It was all falling together. "Sure. The road was deserted last night, remember? It would have been easy for somebody to follow our taillights."

"And see us dumping Jason," Deb said.

"And drag him back off the beach?" Tina asked.

Kelly sighed. "Yes. Of course. Liam, I'm so sorry we doubted you."

He kissed her hand. "Well, looking at this from your side of the fence, I can understand. But now what are you going to do?"

"Get him back," I said.

Liam nodded slowly. "Of course. Do you know where he is?"

"No," Tina said.

We looked around at one another.

"We have to go to Artie again," Tina said. "Maybe he could tell us where Jason is."

"Maybe he doesn't even know what happened," Kelly said.

I leaned forward. "He might not. But he's the only hope we've got. We need to talk to him, but how would we get in to see him? And would he even talk to us again? Remember, our previous encounter with him did not go well."

Deb took a deep breath. "Annie, you and Kelly will have to take another shot at it. He knows you both."

"And probably hates us both," I said.

"Where?" Tina asked, brushing my words aside. "We don't know where he is."

"Probably Southampton Hospital," Liam said.

Kelly whipped out her phone. She clicked away furiously. "Southampton Hospital. Meeting House Lane." She hit a few more buttons and held the phone to her ear. "Yes, I'm checking on a patient there, Arthur Sherman. Is he receiving visitors?" She listened, nodded a few times, and then clicked off her phone. "He's still there. Under observation. And he can receive selected visitors. There's a list."

Deb sighed. "We won't be on it."

"And I also bet there's a guard," I said. *Probably a huge guard*, I thought, *with bulging muscles and a gun.*

"What can I do?" Liam asked.

"Liam, if there's a chance of us getting caught, you should just stay here," Kelly said.

He glanced around. "Do you even have a plan?"

"All we need is his room number," I said. "And a distraction."

"And a lookout person," Tina said. "And someone to stay in the car in case we need to make a quick getaway."

"With Annie and I talking to Artie," Kelly said slowly, "we're out of people." She tilted her head at Liam. "Maybe you should come with us after all."

"Just to drive the car," I said. "That would be safest."

Liam smiled. "Okay, ladies. We can do this."

I was getting very nervous again. "Do we have to?"

Deb nodded. "Yes. I'm afraid we do."

Chapter Eleven

We all went out and down the steps to the cars, but as I pulled the door shut, Liam was right behind me.

"Ah, so Annie, I have a question for you," he said softly.

I was puzzled. "Oh?"

"Yes. About our girl Kelly here. Did she, you know, say anything about me?"

I tried not to grin. I never quite understood what the term *lovesick* meant, but looking at his face, I had a clearer understanding. "Like, in the cafeteria after lunch?"

He wasn't amused. "This is serious. I've been half in love with her for years, you know. I mean, how often does a guy like me get to meet a woman like her? She's perfect. But I keep thinking she's out of my league."

Poor guy. Yes, Kelly was pretty perfect. But she also had a bit of an edge to her that I'd never really noticed until this trip. She may have been worried and scared, but she was also having some fun with this whole situation. She and Liam may have had more in common than I first thought.

"Liam, I hate to sound like a worried parent, but what kind of life could you offer her? Considering your, how shall I put this, involvement with the law?"

He took a very deep breath and exhaled slowly. "Can I swear you to secrecy?"

I worked hard to keep my expression neutral. Was he about to confess? Was this obvious criminal mastermind, hidden away in a corner of Long Island for safety, going to tell me the secret things in his past in an attempt to gain my support? "I swear."

He closed his eyes. "Did you ever hear of Louis 'The Loner' Lamprezzio?"

I thought for a minute, then my brain flooded with a series of images I'd seen on television. Bodies taken from abandoned buildings. Sobbing women. Tight-mouthed wise guys in shiny suits. "Like, six years ago? The US Attorney busted that gang wide open. Were you a member of that, ah, family?"

He rolled his eyes. "Look at me. Do I look Sicilian to you? No. I was the accountant."

I was confused. "Accountant?"

Liam shrugged. "Yeah. Louis never paid taxes, not even on his legit businesses. The Feds came to me and made me an offer."

I cracked a smile. "That you couldn't refuse?"

He didn't crack a smile. "It was either squeal on the biggest mafioso west of Chicago, or they were going to *tell* him I squealed, in which case I was a dead man. So I packed up both sets of books and ran for cover." He put his hand on his heart. "I am, by nature, a very law-abiding citizen."

The horn beeped. Kelly, Tina, and Deb were in the Prius, looking at us expectantly.

"So, yes, you are in the Witness Protection Program, but you're just an accountant?"

He shrugged modestly. "CPA. With an MBA. I do taxes for some of the FBI guys around here, you know? On the side. And I have the vineyard." He leaned in. "I make a good living."

I shook my head. He was obviously very serious about this. "Listen. Liam, this is really crappy timing on your part. But if we make it through the day without being arrested, I'll put in a good word."

He grinned and went down the steps. He gave Kelly a very nice kiss before hopping into the driver's seat of the Prius. We probably would have been more comfortable in the minivan, but my paranoia was running high.

Southampton Hospital was exactly the kind of place I would want to be taken to in a medical emergency. It looked clean and modern. All the cars in the parking lot were shiny and new. It looked like a movie version of a hospital. We parked in the visitors' lot and looked at each other.

"Do we just walk in there and ask for Artie?" I asked.

Deb shook her head. "No. We'll just ask for the room number at the information desk. We can use the stairs. Most hospitals are designed the same way, so the stairs will take us to the end of a hallway instead of directly in front of the nurse's station."

"There has to be another way," I said. "Do we really have to go in there?" My heart hadn't stopped pounding since we'd left the house. I did not want to see Artie again. For a cranky little old man, he'd proven to be shrewd and ruthless. I'd rather be facing my ex-mother-in-law on Thanksgiving afternoon, explaining a half-frozen turkey.

"Annie," Deb said patiently, "we have to find out what happened to Jason. Do you have another idea?"

I shook my head.

Deb shrugged. "See? Artie is our only chance."

I swallowed hard and followed them out of the car.

We walked into the lobby like we knew what we were doing. Deb went up to the reception desk. The lobby carried the movie-set theme even further. Everything was sleek, modern, and beige, with lots of potted plants and very attractive people in wheelchairs. Tina, Kelly, and I kept an eye peeled for men in dark suits. We didn't see any.

"Follow me," Deb said, and we did, down a few hallways and up one flight of stairs. We came out of the stairwell, and there, in a chair outside one of the rooms, was a man in uniform.

We stepped back into the stairwell and closed the door.

I closed my eyes. "Now what?"

Deb was frowning. "We need that distraction," she muttered.

"That's what I'm here for," Tina said.

My eyes flew open. "Tina, wait."

Tina's eyes got real big. "The fact is, this is all my fault. And I have purple hair. I bet if I went up to the guard and started asking questions and being obnoxious, I could get him to follow me."

"But what if he catches you?" I asked.

Tina shrugged. "So, what if he does? If I keep my mouth shut, all they can do is throw me in jail, right? And ladies, if you didn't already know, I've been there before. It's not the worst place in the world to be."

"My, my," Kelly said. "Tina, I must admit, I completely misjudged you."

"Yes, well, I doubled my meds. Let's do this quickly before my real brain starts to do the thinking."

She slipped into the hallway. Deb, Kelly, and I cracked the door and watched through the sliver of the opening.

"Hey," Tina called gaily, "is this Artie Sherman's room?"

The guard stood up. He was actually a police officer. He did not have bulging muscles, but I knew he had to have a gun. He spoke very politely. "Yes, but I'm afraid you have to be on the list to visit him."

She leaned in. "But I'm a fan of Jason Wilde. A *huge* fan." She drummed her fingers along his shoulder. "And if I can just give Artie my phone number, maybe he can pass it along. I'd be *so* grateful. Know what I mean?"

The officer was looking at her very closely. "Miss, can I see some ID?"

"Officer"—she started to giggle—"whatever for?"

The policeman was looking more and more serious. "Please. If I could just see—"

"Never!" Tina shrieked, and started running down the hallway.

And sure enough, the policeman took off after her.

Kelly and I were out of the stairwell and into Artie's room in a heartbeat. Deb stayed outside in the hallway. The curtain was drawn around his bed, and his television was on.

Kelly stepped around the curtain. I was right behind her. Artie was awake, and looked annoyed at Kelly's appearance, but then he saw me and the penny dropped. His jaw sagged open.

"You!"

"Yes, Artie," I said. "We're back."

Kelly snatched the buzzer off the hospital-bed railing. "No need to call for help, Artie," she said. "We just want to chat."

"Officer," Artie called weakly.

"No officer. Sorry. Just us." I sat on the edge of his bed. "Where's Jason?"

Artie stared at me. "Whattaya mean, where's Jason? He's with you."

Kelly shook her head. "No. He's not. We left him in Montauk last night and called the FBI to find him. But when they got to where we'd left him, he had disappeared. Somebody followed us and took Jason off the beach. He's really kidnapped, Artie. And not by us."

Artie's face went white, and he hadn't been looking too great to begin with.

"We think maybe Leo has him now," Kelly said.

Artie covered his eyes with a shaking hand and muttered something. "What?" I asked. I pulled his hand away. "Artie, what do you know?"

He was shaking his head. "Nothin'."

"No," Kelly said. "Something." She dropped her voice. "Do you think your brother could have done this?"

Faintly, I could hear the wail of a police siren. It was time to go. I glanced at Kelly. "Artie, we need to find Jason. And we need you to help us." I shook his shoulder. "Please. I know you would never do anything to hurt him. But I don't know about Leo. There's a lot of money involved."

He covered his face with his hands.

"We don't have any more time," Kelly said, tugging her hair. "Are you really willing to leave Jason with Leo?"

"My brother has a house," Artie muttered. "He and his two grandsons. Arbor Path." He lay back and turned his head.

Kelly and I went to the door to peek into the hallway. Deb was down at one end, and when she saw us, she nodded. We walked calmly back to the stairwell, down and out through the lobby. We didn't speak.

When we stepped outside, Kelly finally burst out, "Where's Tina?"

Deb shook her head. "Don't know. More important, where's Liam?"

We looked into the parking lot. The Prius was not where we'd left it.

"Oh," I whispered. "This isn't good."

The wailing of the police sirens was getting louder. We walked out onto the pavement. Kelly had her phone out when the car swung around from the other side of the building. It was coming in fast. Liam screeched to a halt in front of us, and we piled in. Tina was in the backseat. As we slammed the doors shut, two police cars came speeding up to the entrance, lights blazing. Liam calmly drove past them and into the road.

"Oh, Tina, thank God," Deb said. "I did not want to have to bail you out of jail."

"How," I asked, "did you outrun him in those heels?"

"I didn't," she said. "I let him catch me in the far stairwell, where we were all alone. Then I pretended to faint and started jerking around, like a seizure? So he ran to get help, and I just got off the floor and walked away. Poor guy. He's going to get in trouble. His name was Jerry."

I turned to stare at her. "Are you kidding?"

Tina had her compact out and was fixing her lipstick. "Nope. What did Artie say?"

"Leo has a house," Kelly said. "We have a street but no house number."

"Where is this Arbor Path?" I asked. "Kelly?"

She tapped her phone. "Amagansett. It's a small street. Only about five houses. All woods."

"What should we do?" Tina asked nervously.

"Maybe," Deb said slowly, "we should take a look. Just to see if Artie was telling the truth."

"Guys, I'm not sure we should be playing Nancy Drew," I said. "Maybe what we *should* do is call Andy."

"And tell him what?" asked Tina. "That we didn't kidnap Jason in the first place, but now he's really missing?"

"It might be better," Kelly said, "if we could find Jason, then tell Andy where he is. Then maybe we won't get thrown into prison."

I shook my head. "What do we know about this Leo guy? What if he's dangerous? After all, he is a *real* kidnapper."

Deb waved a hand. "How old is Artie? Sixty-five? And Leo is older. You told us Artie called him the money guy. Probably sits behind a desk all day. There are five of us. Don't you think we can handle one geriatric couch potato and his *grandkids*?"

I wasn't convinced. Of course I wasn't. But what could I do? "Okay. Let's take a look."

Liam turned the car around.

We'd spent lots of time in the past six years driving around looking at the houses of the rich and very rich. Arbor Path fell into the very rich category. No streetlights, and the houses were set so far back from the road they could barely be seen through all the trees.

We pulled over to the side of the road.

"Which house is Leo's?" Tina finally asked.

Deb shrugged. "Who knows? Maybe we should go up to each one of them. Pretend we're lost and ask for directions?"

I groaned. "That's the best you can come up with. We're *lost*?"

Deb threw me a look. "Any better ideas?"

"Wait," Liam said.

A car pulled out of one of the driveways—a new white Cadillac. There were three men inside. It headed out toward the main road.

"That's the car," Tina said excitedly.

"Then let's start with that house," Kelly said. "It looks like Leo and the boys just made a bagel run."

"We can go up and see if we can look in any windows," I said. "Liam, pull up to the end of the street. If you see them coming back, call. Deb, Kelly, let's see if we can peek in the windows. Everyone got their phone?"

"Oh, my God, guys," Kelly said, slipping her phone into the pocket of her jeans. "What if they come back?"

Deb opened the door and hopped out. "Easy," she said. "We can just go through the woods back to the main road."

Tina started whining. "Why do I have to stay with the car?"

"Because," Deb said, "you're wearing those idiotic shoes. How are you supposed to run through the woods in heels?"

Tina got into the front seat and the Prius pulled away. Kelly and I followed Deb up the gravel drive.

"What if there are more people at the house?" I asked. I did not have a good feeling about this.

"We'll ring the bell. If no one answers, we'll have a look around," Kelly said.

"Kelly, how long have you wanted to be a spy?"

She grinned. "Come on, this is kind of fun."

Deb nodded. "Yeah. It really is."

No, it was not fun. We were about to add breaking and entering to our long line of offenses. How could they be talking about *fun*?

The house was gorgeous. Lots of windows, no drapes. As long as Jason was on the first floor, we'd be able to see him from the front porch. The drive went around the back of the house, probably to a garage. We followed a slate walkway to the front door.

Deb rang the bell a few times. It was very quiet. There was the sound of birds and crickets but nothing else. After a minute or two, we started around to the back of the house.

The pool was also gorgeous. Lots of expensive outdoor wicker, and pots of palm trees and ferns. More floor-to-ceiling windows. More chirping of birds. We looked in all the windows. Very modern—sleek furniture and abstract art. And, in the corner bedroom, a naked blond man asleep in a king-size bed.

"Yes," Deb crowed. "Score!"

"Okay," I said. "We found him. Let's go."

"We should make sure he's okay," Kelly said.

"How?" I asked. "You mean, you want to go in the house? Are you *crazy?*"

Deb ignored me. She tried the sliding glass door. It opened easily. We walked into the bedroom and stood over Jason's unconscious form. He was snoring. Deb checked his pulse and pried open his eyes. She peeled off the patch.

"He's fine," Deb said. She began to wander around the room. "Would you look at this closet? It's bigger than my bedroom!"

"This is where Leo is staying?" Kelly said. "Then why was Artie in a crummy hotel?"

"He *said* he was in a crummy hotel," I reminded her. "We only had his word for it. And his word was not exactly golden."

Kelly nodded. "True. Well, we should probably let Andy know where he can find the famously missing Jason Wilde."

"We should probably get the hell out of Dodge," I said.

"Relax, Annie," Kelly said. "The bad guys are gone. We're fine. Call."

"Should I have him come here?" I asked.

Deb frowned. "It might be easier to explain things to him first."

I nodded and pulled my phone out of my jeans and dialed. "Andy? Listen, I know you're probably very busy, but I really need to talk to you. In person. As soon as possible."

There was silence. Then, "This sounds serious."

I swallowed hard. "It kinda is."

"I'm a little involved right now," he said. "Where are you?"

"In Amagansett. Past the country club out there?"

"I'm at Southampton Hospital right now. I could be tied up all day."

Of course. They were talking to Artie Sherman. I cleared my throat. "Artie isn't going to tell you anything that I can't tell you myself. Trust me."

More silence. "Annie? What could you possibly know about Artie Sherman and what he can or can't tell me?"

I closed my eyes. "Because I already talked to him."

"Where are you?"

"I told you. Amagansett."

"There's a place called the Old Stone Market," he said. His voice was suddenly very cold. "Do you know it?"

"No, but we can find it."

"We?"

I opened my eyes. Kelly and Deb were watching me closely. "Tina and I. My skinny, purple-haired friend, Tina."

"It will take me about forty minutes," he said. His voice was completely neutral. He could have been talking to a stranger. "And I'll be bringing some of my coworkers."

"That's fine," I said.

"I thought you weren't going to break my heart," he said very softly.

I felt something catch in my throat. "I'm not going to. Honestly."

He hung up.

"You okay?" Kelly asked.

I stared at the phone in my hand. Were those tears I felt? How did this happen? I barely knew this man. I wasn't in love with him. I couldn't be.

But he represented something almost as important as love. The possibility. The promise. The idea that my life didn't have to be settled, and that amazing things could still happen.

I took a ragged breath. We'd be fine, I told myself. Once he knew the truth, we'd be just fine.

"I'm good," I said rather loudly. I glanced around. "So, can we go now?"

"And leave him here?" Kelly asked.

"Yes, leave him here," I hissed. "Unless we want to drag him out to the street and throw him in the trunk of the Prius. Let's go."

"I really need to pee," Deb said.

"What? Now?" I asked. Honestly, her bladder was the size of a lima bean.

She gave me a look and headed for the bathroom. She was in there less than a minute when she popped her head out. "You guys gotta see this," she said. "It's bigger than my whole first floor."

Yes, I know. Probably not the best time to take a tour, but Kelly and I walked in. The bathroom was all white tile and gleaming chrome.

The soaker tub was the size of your average hot tub. The shower was big enough to walk in to. With the entire Ohio State marching band.

My phone made a noise. A text. From Tina.

Get out.

I felt a sudden chill. "They're coming back," I said.

Deb looked up from shaking the water from her hands. "Well, that certainly wasn't a very long trip. Where did they—"

She froze. We heard the distinct sound of a garage door being opened.

I looked around in panic. "We need to run."

Kelly shook her head. "No. We need to hide. Come on in here."

There was a linen closet next to the shower. And all three of us fit inside. It was very dark and smelled faintly of lavender. Quite cozy, actually.

We strained to hear anything, but whoever came back either moved quietly or had fallen asleep in the garage.

"What do we do now?" Kelly whispered.

Good question. The easiest thing would be to simply walk out of the bathroom and through the glass doors to freedom. The problem there was that anyone inside the house could see us, and might wonder what the heck three women were doing sneaking around the pool.

I texted Tina:

We may need another diversion.

Deb sighed. "Do you think that's wise?"

"How else are we going to get out of here?" I whispered. "We can't just walk out the way we came in."

I opened the closet door. There was complete silence. We crept across the bathroom. The door was open to the bedroom, and we could see Jason, lying peacefully unaware. There was still no noise. Where were these guys?

Kelly gripped my hand. "Annie, I'm scared," she breathed.

I was scared too. Yes, Leo may have been old. And probably not much of a threat. But his grandsons were with him. They weren't old. Maybe they were twelve, but they looked a lot older than that when they passed us in their Caddy. And now, there were only three of us. Everything had suddenly gone from The Hopewell Ladies' Excellent Adventure to an episode of Mission: Impossible.

There were voices outside. Deb cautiously moved toward the glass doors, looked, and then quickly came back to us.

"They're by the pool. It looks like lunchtime. We can go out the front," she said calmly.

"Front?" I squeaked. Who leaves the house they just broke into by the *front door*?

Deb nodded. "Tell Tina to be ready to go."

I texted as we moved out of the bedroom into the hallway. My heart was pounding so loudly I was sure Leo could hear it, even if he was poolside. We tiptoed past open doorways and into a vast foyer. The view of the woods was magnificent. I stopped to stare at the expanse of trees and flowering shrubs. Then I focused on three men, sitting in the expensive wicker, half-hidden by the palms, eating sandwiches. Leo and the boys, happily munching away. They never glanced in our direction. Why should they? I don't think I was breathing as we slipped out the front door and raced down the gravel driveway.

The car was waiting for us. The side door was open, and we tumbled inside, barely closing it as Liam raced away. I glanced back. The garage door was open, the white Caddy inside, but no one was following us.

"Well?" Tina asked.

"He's there," Kelly said, gasping for air. "Still out cold."

"And naked?" Tina asked.

I exhaled very loudly. I hadn't realized how scared I was until I felt all the muscles in my neck suddenly loosen and tears welled up in my eyes. "What if they had found us?"

Kelly hugged me. "They didn't. What did Andy say?"

I gulped and choked back my tears. "We need to find the Old Stone Market."

Liam had been driving back the way we came, but pulled over to the side of the road. He shut off the car. "What are we doing next? Because I gotta tell you, I'm ready to just head for Canada and pray for the best."

"Andy is meeting me," I said. "We know where Jason is. We'll explain what happened, he'll rescue Jason, and everything will be just fine."

"Sure," Deb said. "As long as Leo stays put. And Jason stays put. What if they decide to take Jason for a joyride? Then we're totally screwed."

I glanced at Kelly. Her eyes were closed, and her forehead wrinkled. "You're a bit of a Debbie Downer today. Well, every day," she finally said.

Deb's shoulders slumped. "Yeah? So?"

"There's no reason for them to go anywhere," Kelly said, irritated. "And we're meeting Andy in—" She glanced at me.

"Twenty minutes," I said.

"Besides," Kelly said firmly, "they were having lunch. I say we're safe. Annie, we'll drop you off to talk to Andy. Then Liam and I will come back here and stake out the house. If they go anywhere, we'll just follow them. Simple."

Stakeout? Follow them? Good Lord, we'd become Charlie's Angels.

Kelly had her phone out. "The Old Stone Market is just up the road. In the other direction. Just turn us around, Liam, and we should be there in, like, five minutes."

We found the market with no problem. I got out of the car and looked around. The place was open but quiet, and the parking lot was empty.

"Do you want me to stay with you?" Deb asked.

I nodded.

"Me too?" Tina was already out of the front seat. "After all, I'm the one who started this whole mess. Kind of."

We slammed the car door shut and watched Liam and Kelly head back toward Arbor Path.

There were outdoor tables, and the sun was shining, so I sat down and tried not to feel like I was a ten-year-old waiting outside the principal's office. Tina wandered off into the market. Deb sat beside me and patted me on the knee.

"I know that you and Andy will be just fine," she said.

"I've been lying to him," I said.

"Yes, but only to protect the rest of us. He'll understand."

"You heard what Liam said. He's a big deal. He takes his job very seriously. And, basically, I'm a wanted criminal."

"But once you explain everything, you'll practically be a hero. After all, we have solved the *real* kidnapping."

"Which never would have happened in the first place if we hadn't . . . if Tina hadn't . . . whatever."

"Exactly," Deb said. "Whatever. But none of it was really our fault. Well, Tina's fault, maybe, but the rest was just crazy circumstance."

"He asked me not to break his heart," I said, staring down at my feet.

"Oh, Annie, how sweet! Don't worry. You won't," Deb said.

Tina returned with a small brown paper bag.

"Cookie?" She thrust the bag at me. Something wonderful and chocolaty hit my nose, and my stomach rumbled. I pulled out a huge chocolate-chip cookie, still warm, and nibbled. Anytime was the right time for a little stress eating.

"Leo and his sons were just here," Tina said matter-of-factly. "They've been coming here all week, getting takeout. The owner said they were nasty and cheap and not very talkative, but they said they'd be leaving tonight."

I froze, midchew.

"She also said that Leo asked about renting a boat."

I glanced at my watch again. Andy needed to know this. Where was he?

A few moderate-size bites of cookie later, his car pulled into the lot, followed by two black SUVs filled with men wearing sunglasses. When he said he would bring some of his coworkers, he wasn't kidding. He'd brought an entire battalion.

He got out of the car, shut the door quietly, and straightened his tie. The SUVs both stopped, windows open, engines idling.

I took a deep breath.

Showtime.

Chapter Twelve

He walked slowly over to the bench and sat beside me. His eyes never left my face.

"Annie?"

I cleared my throat. "Andy, these are two friends of mine," I said. "Tina here, and Deb."

His eyes narrowed. He turned to stare at Tina.

She raised her hand and waggled her fingers. "Nice to meet you, Andy."

I grabbed his hand, and his eyes moved back to mine. "I need to tell you what happened Monday night. At the American Hotel," I said.

There was a beat. "You were at the American on Monday night?" he asked.

"Yes," I said. "We were with Jason Wilde."

To his credit, he did not withdraw his hand.

Tina smiled at him. "You see, I'm a big fan of Jason's, and the bartender had told us that he usually came in, so we were just kind of sitting around, waiting for him, and he came in and had a few drinks with us."

"The problem was," I said, leaning forward, "that he was on a Fentanyl patch. That is a narcotic, and should never, ever be taken with alcohol. Of course, Jason ignored that and drank anyway. So he was in serious trouble, sobrietywise."

"Yes," Tina said. "He obviously couldn't drive, and he said he was staying on Dune Road, so we offered to take him home. Unfortunately, before he could tell us *where* on Dune Road, he completely passed out. So we brought him into the house so he could sleep it off."

Andy's jaw unclenched, but barely. "That is *almost* believable. But what happened the next morning?"

"Well," I said, "we tried to wake him up. But . . ."

Andy nodded. "I understand the part where you couldn't wake him up." His eyes were very cold. "Can you explain why you didn't just call the police?"

Tina raised her hand. "My fault. Jason put out a restraining order against me. They didn't want to get me in trouble."

Andy shifted his weight and leaned forward. His hand left mine. He looked, if possible, even more official. "Restraining order?"

Tina waved her hands carelessly. "It was years ago. But the thing is, they didn't call the police as a favor to me."

"And we didn't know he was going to be passed out for so long," I said. "Until Deb looked at him, and then—"

"Wait." Andy held out both hands, as if to stop a charging bull. "Deb?"

"Me. We've never actually met, but I admired your shoes at John Scott's. I'm a nurse," Deb explained, smiling. "Once I saw the patch, I knew he'd be out for a while."

"And?" Andy asked. I kept looking for some warmth or humor in his handsome face, but he looked deadly serious and completely unsympathetic.

"Then Artie called Jason. We answered the phone, told Artie what happened, and Artie told us he'd take care of everything," I explained. "But instead of fixing things, he concocted a plan."

"Artie wanted to capitalize on Jason's disappearance," Tina said. "He wanted the publicity. I've never met Artie, by the way, but I don't think he's very trustworthy."

"Artie was born a snake," Deb said. "But we had no idea. We thought he was telling everyone that Jason was fine."

Andy tilted his head and frowned slightly. "Jason was where?"

"In the bedroom," I told him. "With Muffy."

He closed his eyes a moment. "Muffy?"

"The dog," I explained. "Tina's dog."

Tina dimpled. "She's such a sweetheart."

"So," he asked slowly, "Jason was in on this?"

"After he woke up, he called Artie, who told him that being missing was the best thing that had happened to his career in years. Then, I guess Artie concocted the kidnapping idea," I said.

"Of course it was Artie's idea. Jason couldn't think of something like that on his best day," Deb said.

"It meant more publicity," I continued. "National publicity. He told Jason to stay right where he was. Sadly, Jason always does exactly what Artie tells him to do. So he wasn't moving out of the house until Artie gave the word."

"So he was there when my men came to your house?" Andy asked. "What happened when they saw your car?"

"Well," Deb explained, "we switched the Jersey plates with the rental-car plates."

Andy nodded. I saw a flicker of something like admiration in his eyes, and felt a bit of weight lift from my heart. "Good move. Where did you get a rental car? We sent out your descriptions right away."

"Right in town," I said. "Deb wasn't with us, you see, at the American. So Liam drove us, and she was able to get the rental."

He closed his eyes again. "Liam?"

"Yes. He's a sommelier at the Milland Vineyard," I said.

"You mean, Liam O'Donnell?" Andy asked, his eyes opening wide.

"Maybe," Deb said. "We don't know his last name. But he's in the Witness Protection Program."

Andy opened his mouth to say something, stopped, then tried again. "Did he tell you that?"

"No," I said. "But we figured it out ourselves." I smiled brightly. Now that I knew the truth about Liam, I was doubly proud of our deductive reasoning. He wasn't an actual criminal, of course, but still.

Andy stared at a point right over my left shoulder. "Did Artie send the note?"

"Yes," I said. "But it was his brother Leo's idea."

Andy slowly nodded, eyes half-closed. "That makes sense," he muttered. "Of course." He looked up. "How did you get Artie to meet you at the bar?" he asked.

Deb waved a hand. "We tracked Artie down ourselves. We wanted him to take Jason off our hands."

"*You* tracked Artie down?" Andy asked. There was not quite so much disbelief in his voice. Was it possible he was going to believe us?

I lifted my chin. "We found out where he was hanging out, and waited for him. But instead of being cooperative, he went all crazy ninja on us."

"Crazy ninja?" Andy repeated faintly.

"Yes," I said. "He started yelling and jumping around." I leaned toward Andy. "We did not have a gun. And we did not touch him. At all."

Andy sat there for what seemed to be a very long time before he sighed and said, "I believe you. So then what?"

"Then we told Jason he was outta there," I said. "So last night, we put together a plan. We put the Fentanyl patch back on him and had him drink a bit. We drove him out to Montauk. Once he passed out, we left him naked on the beach, and called the hotline anonymously so somebody could pick him up."

"Wait." Andy held up his hands again. "Why did you drug him?"

"That was going to be his story," Tina explained. "That he had been drugged most of the time, and he didn't remember anything."

"Uh-huh." Andy made a face. "Of course. And naked?"

"No DNA," I said. "Or fibers."

"Ah. Yes, well, that makes sense too. So you're the one who called the hotline?"

I nodded.

"I have one question. Why wasn't he on the beach when we went there?"

"Leo took him," Deb explained. "He knew where Jason was, you see. There was a GPS thingy on Jason's phone. Artie and Leo knew where he was the whole time. So he staked out our place."

"As bad guys do," Tina put in.

"Or, I don't know, maybe one of his grandsons did, and then followed us and grabbed Jason off the beach." Deb lifted her shoulders and let them drop. "As bad guys do."

"And how do you know this?"

"Because we went back to Artie," I told him.

"Aha," he said. "So, that *was* you at the hospital?"

"Yes," I said. "And Artie told us that Leo and his grandsons had a house and that's where Jason was."

Andy clenched his jaw and nodded several times to himself. "I don't think that Leo is as harmless as everyone thinks he is. His son is a very dangerous man. He's been indicted several times for fraud, extortion, and assault. The two boys are just as bad. They're all connected, somehow, and have always managed to get off. They would have no problem kidnapping Wilde for five million dollars. They would also have no qualms about killing him." He looked around and exhaled loudly. "We need to get back to Artie and find out where they are."

"Um, Andy? They're right down the road. A house on Arbor Path," I told him.

"Artie told you that?" he asked, eyes wide.

"Not willingly."

He stood up. "We'll need to confirm," he muttered, taking out his phone.

"Um, we did that too," I said.

He froze, and looked at me with narrowed eyes. "What?"

"We went to Arbor Path," I explained. "And when they left the house—"

"For lunch," Tina interrupted. "And they came here. You need to talk to the owner of this place about the boat."

"Boat?"

"Yes," I said. "But when they left the house, we snuck around back and found Jason. He's in the back bedroom. We went in to check on him. He's still out cold."

"You went in?" He threw his hands up in the air. "Are you crazy? Those men would have thought nothing about killing you all if they'd found you."

"Well, we didn't know that," I explained patiently. "How could we know that?" My phone suddenly chirped. I pulled it out and saw a text from Kelly.

```
They just put Jason in the trunk. Looks
like they're heading out. Where is Andy?
```

"Andy, we need to do something. Leo is on the move."

"How do you know that?"

"We left Liam and Kelly at the house," I said. "They're in the rental car. Watching."

Andy stood up. "Mitchell," he yelled, "get to Arbor Path." He looked down at me. "I don't suppose you know what kind of car they're driving?"

I stood up next to him and yelled. "White Caddy, Mitchell."

An SUV peeled out of the drive and raced away.

I dialed Kelly. "Well?"

"They're at the main road, hold on . . . going north," she said. "On Old Stone Highway."

I looked up and, sure enough, a white Cadillac sped by. Followed by the rented Prius.

I pointed. Andy whipped his head around and moved toward his car.

This would have been the point where I would have gratefully watched somebody else take care of the rest of this mess. But those were my friends following the Caddy.

And there was Andy. I could not bear the thought of him driving away without me. What if he never came back?

So I moved.

"Are you kidding?" he yelped as I reached for the passenger-side door.

I jumped into the seat and strapped myself in. He got in beside me.

"Get out," he said.

"Make me."

"You can't be here," he said, somewhat strongly.

"I have to be."

"This could be dangerous."

"You can't protect me?"

"Are you always this difficult?"

"No. Maybe. We gonna follow these guys or what?"

He swore. He banged on the steering wheel with both hands.

Then he turned out onto Old Stone Highway.

I had never been in a high-speed chase before. Not that it started out that way. We were just following the Prius, and behind us was the other SUV. Andy had Bluetooth, of course, and started barking out orders the minute we got on the road. I'd told Andy which house on Arbor Path was Leo's, and Team Mitchell was to secure it. Team Felder, following us, was to keep a safe distance. I called Kelly, and she and Liam exited Old Stone Highway at the first turnoff so that Andy and I were directly behind Leo and company, although several yards back.

There was a lull. I cleared my throat. "Do you believe our story, Andy?"

I was afraid to look at him, but when I did, he was actually smiling. "Annie, I can't imagine anyone making up a story as crazy as this one. As soon as Jason gives his statement, you all will be in a much better place. Yes, I believe you. But you'll still have to come down and make a statement."

I almost melted into the seat from relief.

"But that doesn't mean there may not be consequences. Faking a kidnapping is also a crime. Somebody will have to answer for it."

I stared straight ahead, trying not to think who that somebody would be.

Someone called in to Andy. The house on Arbor Path was empty. Andy gave orders for one agent to stay at the house. The rest of Team Mitchell was coming up behind us. Andy clenched his jaw again.

He was muttering. "Where the hell are they taking him?"

"What's ahead?" I asked.

He shrugged. "The ocean."

I dialed Tina. "Hey, go in and find out all you can about that boat Leo wanted. Call me back right away."

"Yeah, what was that about a boat?" Andy asked.

"Leo asked about renting one."

He swore under his breath and started giving orders again. Apparently, every federal agent on the Eastern Seaboard was now heading in our direction.

"It doesn't make sense," Andy muttered. "There's just canoes and kayaks up this way. What were they going to rent?"

"Not to worry. Tina's on the case."

He glanced over. "So, I guess going forward, you aren't going to have too many issues about my job being, ah, dangerous?"

Going forward? Did he really just say that? I tried to keep my grin to a minimum. "I never thought of myself as the danger-loving type. This is definitely a new side to my personality."

"Do not," he said, "let yourself get too carried away."

Tina called me back. I listened, and then relayed the information, trying to keep my voice from shaking.

"Andy, the owner at the market? She overheard Leo. He wanted a small boat that he and his sons could take out to the middle of the bay. They only wanted it for a few hours."

He swore. "Did she know who he was talking too?"

"Tina says no. He just had a list of boat rentals in the area."

"Mitchell, Felder," he said, loudly. "They're planning to dump Wilde out into the bay. We need to take them now."

He tightened his grip on the steering wheel. I could see the white Caddy ahead of us. Our car started gaining speed. Behind us, I could hear sirens.

The Caddy took off like a shot. Andy swore and stomped on the accelerator. I was suddenly afraid. Up until now, I'd pretended that Andy and I were just out for a ride. At ninety miles per hour, it became something else. I huddled back and closed my eyes, my hands clenching the sides of my seat.

So, being in a high-speed car chase involved lots of swearing on the part of the driver. In Andy's case, I suppose I should have felt gladdened by the fact that he was so comfortable in my company that he used words and phrases that, ordinarily, would be confined to porn-movie scripts. I occasionally opened my eyes to see trees and things whipping by so fast that I closed my eyes again quickly to avoid vertigo. Andy kept up a steady stream of conversation with his men, as well as the aforementioned not-so-inner dialogue.

My eyes were shut when we swerved and the road got significantly bumpier. I took a quick peek. It looked like Leo had decided to go four-wheeling in his shiny Cadillac, because we were in the woods, dodging trees, and bouncing over small bushes. Ahead I could see clear-blue sky that meant only one thing—open water.

I looked behind us. Both black SUVs were bringing up the rear. I could hear more sirens. Leo had nowhere to go.

The Caddy stopped suddenly. It had to. It had come to a clearing that led into the bay. Andy hit the brakes, and we bounced hard as we slowed down. A young man was getting out of the Caddy. He jerked open the back door of the car and pulled someone out, a struggling figure whose head was covered by a towel. By the time we came to a stop at the edge of the clearing, Leo, bald and in khakis and a loud Hawaiian shirt, was standing beside the younger man. Leo had a gun, and was pointing it at the figure now motionless on the ground.

Andy turned off his car and took a deep breath. He opened the door very cautiously, then glared back at me.

"Don't even move," he whispered.

He approached Leo slowly, with both his hands spread wide in the air.

"Leo Sherman? I'm Agent Mooney. FBI. Let's not make this any worse than it already is."

I looked behind me. Both SUVs were parked behind us, doors open, agents poised with their guns all pointing at Leo.

"Come any closer and I'll kill him." Leo called. "In fact, if you all don't turn around in the next three minutes, I'll kill him."

Andy stopped. "Leo, like I said, we don't want to make this any worse."

"No, we don't," Leo called. "So turn around and get the hell out of here."

What was wrong with this picture? Leo and his grandson. But where was Grandson Number Two?

I called quietly. "Ah, Andy?"

He didn't hear me. There was lots of chatter in the background—sirens getting closer, voices back and forth, the radio cackling.

I got out of the car and circled around the back and up behind Andy.

He glanced back at me. "Are you kidding?" he hissed.

"They put Jason in the trunk," I whispered, and then backed away.

His shoulders relaxed. He looked back at his team and waved them forward. "Let's go. Let's take these guys."

Leo shook the gun. "Are you crazy? I'll blow his head off."

Andy shrugged elaborately. "Hey, if you want to blow the head off your own grandson, go right ahead."

Leo slowly dropped the gun.

The man on the ground stood up and pulled the towel off his head. "I told you this was a stupid idea," he screamed at Leo.

"Don't blame me," Leo screamed back, pointing to the driver of the car. "This is all your idiot brother's fault."

Men in black suits swarmed Leo and his grandsons. Handcuffs appeared. Police cars pulled up. Things suddenly got loud and confusing.

Andy reached into the Caddy and popped open the trunk. I ran forward and stood next to him as he opened it.

There, wrapped in a sheet, was Jason Wilde. He was barely awake. He licked his lips and tried to speak.

"Annie?"

"Yep. It's all good, Jason. You're safe."
He closed his eyes and half smiled.
And drooled just a little.

I expected to be politely escorted to some stark concrete building where I'd be carefully questioned for several hours by a black-suited stranger who would listen to every word of my story, then ask me to repeat it twenty more times, waiting for me to either slip up or break down completely, confessing finally to not only kidnapping, but also torture, attempted murder, and unethical sexual congress with a federal agent.

As it was, Andy followed us all back to Dune Road, where his minions sat around and took statements from us and waited while Jason, Leo, and Leo's grandsons told their stories from wherever they'd been taken.

The press had gotten wind of the chase and were camping out at the hospital when Jason was delivered by ambulance. Jason managed to wave at the crowd before being wheeled into the ER, causing every news truck and freelance reporter to rush Southampton like the Missouri Land Grab. Andy had not been pleased with that. Neither was his immediate superior, who arrived later in the afternoon with news.

"Jason Wilde says he was drugged throughout his entire captivity and doesn't remember anything," Agent Delmonico said. He had been introduced as Special Agent Delmonico from the New York City branch office, and I assumed he was one of Andy's "big guns."

I nodded. "Of course. That's exactly what we told him to say. Did you tell him exactly what happened? How Leo grabbed him?"

Delmonico nodded.

"And did you tell him he didn't need to fall back on his cover story, but that he needed to tell the truth?" I continued.

Agent Delmonico folded his hands on his lap. "Why did he need a cover story?"

We had given out individual statements and were now sitting as a group in the living room.

"Well," Kelly said, "we didn't want to get into any trouble, so we thought if he could just play like he was drugged the whole time, he wouldn't have to be forced to try to identify any of us."

I'm not sure if Delmonico had read any of our statements, but he and Andy had a brief powwow in the small bedroom before he came out to talk to us.

"In fact," Delmonico said, "he's denying he's ever been here. His story is that he had a drink with you, left the bar, and remembers nothing else."

Deb sighed. "We should have known. The man is an idiot. He's going to send us all to jail through sheer stubbornness and stupidity."

"Perhaps," Kelly suggested, "we could go over there and see if we can, well, jog his memory?"

"I think not," Delmonico said.

"What about Artie?" I asked. "He knows what really happened."

Delmonico nodded briefly. "Arthur Sherman has indeed made a very long and detailed statement. Which is why you all are here instead of in a holding cell."

At that moment, Liam and Agent Felder came in from the deck. They had originally greeted each other like old friends, and they had been out there for quite some time.

Liam crouched down by Kelly. "You doing okay, darlin'?"

Kelly kissed him lightly on the lips. "Yes, thanks, Liam. Did you tell the nice man about how you found Jason when you were here? And how he was here of his own free will? And how we were desperately trying to get rid of him?"

Liam stood up and smiled at Andy. "Ah, Agent Mooney. Good to see you again. And this gentleman, would he be the famous Agent Delmonico?"

Delmonico frowned. "And who are you?"

"Liam O'Donnell. At least, that's the name your generous cohorts gave me."

Delmonico's face cleared. "Ah. Yes. Are you involved with this, ah, situation?"

Liam nodded. "Indeed. Sammy and I have had a very long conversation on the subject, and he seems to think a formal statement is in order. But trust me, these ladies are victims of bizarre circumstance and extreme bad luck, that's all."

He winked at Kelly and grinned.

Delmonico stood up and looked at Andy, somewhat coolly. "You'll keep me informed?"

Andy nodded and walked out with him. Several agents followed, leaving us alone, except for Felder and Liam.

"If I don't eat soon," Kelly said, "I'm going to faint."

I jumped up. "Me too. What's left in the fridge?"

Not too much, as it turned out, but when Andy came back into the house, he looked at the counter and shook his head. "How much time do you all spend eating anyway?"

Deb was arranging some salami and crackers on a paper plate. "Not as often as we'd like on this trip. We've been forced to stay here. We never even made it to Nick & Toni's."

I looked at Andy. "Well?"

Andy shrugged. "When Artie heard that his brother was intending to let Jason sink to the bottom of the bay, he spilled his guts. He pretty much confirmed everything you all said."

Kelly delicately sipped her beer. "Are we going to be arrested?"

Andy shook his head. "I don't think so. For one thing, I don't know what they'd charge you with."

"Total stupidity?" Deb suggested.

Andy laughed. "That's not against the law. Not yet, anyway. Besides, you ladies weren't stupid. You figured out what was going on way before we did."

"Well, it helps when the victim of the crime is crashing in your bedroom," I said.

"True." He sighed. "We'll try to find an official story for the press. After all, we need to explain why you were all over the news. Our best idea so far is that you all met Jason at the American, offered him a ride home, and left him in front of his house. Leo was waiting for him down the road, drove up after you left, and picked him up. That's actually very close to the truth, without all the stuff in between where he was living here like a long-lost son."

"What about the scene at the bar?" Kelly asked. "We were all over the news then too."

Andy shrugged. "I'm sure we can get Artie to admit that you were, indeed, just an actress he had promised to put in the show. And when you hunted him down, he panicked and went, all, what was that phrase? Crazy ninja?"

He smiled at me, and my heart jumped.

"I need to get Mr. O'Donnell to the office for a statement," Agent Felder said very formally.

"Ah, Sammy, can we stop for a bit of somethin' somethin' on the way in?" Liam asked, picking at the salami and crackers.

Andy shook his head. "No. This is an official investigation, not old home week. I'll go with you." He looked down at me. "Can I come back when I'm through?"

I nodded.

"Even if it's late?"

I nodded again.

He smiled. "Good," he said, and they all left.

We found our seats around the table and ate in silence. I felt tired to the bone, but my mind was racing so fast I couldn't imagine ever sleeping again.

"Well, this was some exciting vacation," Deb said at last.

Tina had rescued Muffy, who'd been shut in the bathroom during the FBI occupation. She now fed the growling dog a bit of sliced turkey. "Do you think *People* magazine will want to interview us?"

I stared at her. "About what?"

Tina fluttered her hand. "About all of this."

"I don't think," Kelly said slowly, "anyone is going to question the official story here. We're just going to be the women who drove Jason to meet his kidnapper. I'm betting *People* won't be interested."

Tina made a pouty face. "But this is all about us as much as it is about him."

"And do you think for one second," I said, "that Jason's going to let any bit of attention move from him to us? I bet he'll claim he never even knew our names."

"Exactly," Kelly said. "Nobody is going to know we had anything to do with this unless we tell them. And you know, Tina, what happens on Dune Road . . ."

". . . stays on Dune Road," we all said, Tina included.

Tina sighed and rubbed noses with Muffy. "Our little secret," she whispered.

It was after midnight.

Deb had been in bed for hours. Kelly, Tina, and I watched the continual loop of Jason's rescue by the stalwart members of the FBI and Suffolk County law enforcement. No mention was made of any tourists from New Jersey.

Andy and Liam finally returned. Tina was told that Jason's girl-friend had set up permanent camp in his hospital room, and he had no interest in seeing her again. She looked disappointed and scurried off to bed with Muffy in tow.

Kelly and Liam declared they were going off for a walk, even though the temperature had dropped and the wind had picked up.

I waved tiredly as they left. "Stay up on the dunes," I called faintly. Liam grinned wickedly as he shut the sliding glass door behind him.

Andy sat next to me on the couch, leaning forward, his forearms balanced on his knees. He looked exhausted, but there was a nervous energy about him, and he drummed his fingertips together.

"What's going to happen to Artie?"

Andy shrugged. "He cut a deal. Leo and his grandsons will face charges, but Artie should end up with a slap on the wrist. And your boy Jason will probably get a new contract and maybe a movie deal out of this whole thing."

"And you?" I glanced at him. He was wearing his thinking face.

"I might get a promotion," he said. "Or they'll send me to an outpost in Alaska. I'm not quite sure how this is to all shake out."

"Oh?"

"But wherever I go, it probably won't be New Jersey."

I could feel my blood starting to pound. "Oh?"

He looked up at me and smiled tiredly. "Oh? Is that all you have to say?"

"Do you hate me for lying to you and messing up your case and almost ruining your entire career?"

He threw back his head and laughed. "Good Lord, woman, you are really something else. I was going to say thank you."

"Oh, Andy, don't thank me. After all, we really didn't do anything. Well, actually, we did everything. I mean, if it weren't for us, none of this would have happened. But once it did happen, you would have figured everything out. Yes, we did tell you where Jason was, and what car to follow. And if it weren't for us, you might have spent hours in a hostage negotiation with Leo over his own grandson. But Jason would have been found safe, even without us butting in."

He shook his head. "I meant, thank you for not breaking my heart.

I stared down at my shoes. "Oh."

"Do you think we could handle a long-distance thing?"

I swallowed hard. "Not if you're in Alaska. I mean, I would never willingly travel to a place that's actually *colder* than where I'm living now, even for a visit. In the summer, maybe, but I really don't like to fly. Besides, people up there eat *whale*."

He reached over and grabbed my hand in both of his. "I'm thinking if I stayed right here, things wouldn't be too bad."

I looked up at him. His eyes were shining.

"Are you kidding?" I said. "I love it out here. And it's an easy commute."

"Yes. And I can see all the treasures of Hopewell."

I nudged him with my elbow. "You've already seen all the treasures of Hopewell. We're as good as it gets."

"I believe you. We could see how it goes for a while, you know?"

"That sounds good."

"Eventually, though, you might have to move out here," he said.

"That's a pretty big *might*."

"Yes, it is. And that would mean leaving all your friends behind in Hopewell. Do you think you could do that?"

"Gosh, let me think. Stay in Hopewell with my friends and drive out here on weekends, or live out here full-time and let *them* do the driving? I'm going to have to really think about that. Hmm . . . okay, I've thought about it. No problem."

"Are your kids going to be okay with this?"

"I'm a big girl. They stopped telling me what to do years ago."

He laughed.

Remember how I said I didn't believe in love at first sight? I still didn't. But I had known him almost a whole week now, and whatever I was feeling was way beyond simple lust.

I leaned over until our faces were close. I brushed his lips very lightly with my own. "Upstairs, there are candles."

"Yes?"

I nodded. "Yes. And Marvin Gaye is on my iPod."

He raised an eyebrow. "Is that significant?"

"Very. Now, I must admit, our impromptu session on the dunes was quite the showstopper, but I have something very special planned. And planning is what I do best."

He grinned. "Is that so?"

I grinned back. "Yes. But I'm also getting pretty good at doing."

I grabbed his hand and led him upstairs. I'd tell you all about what happened next, but you know what they say about what happens on Dune Road . . .

Acknowledgments

As always, I would like to thank Lynn Seligman for her constant belief in my work, as well as all her advice. She is always my first defense against a bad book.

I would also like to thank Tiffany Yates-Martin and Cheryl Murphy for helping me get the manuscript into such good shape.

A special shout-out to Patrick Dugan for helping me round out Andy's rough edges, and turning him into a real FBI agent.

A tip of the hat to Ray at the American Hotel, for making the best whiskey sour I have ever tasted.

Many hugs to Danielle Marshall of Lake Union Publishing for saying yes, and really "getting" everything I wanted to say in this book.

And for all my readers out there, your support has meant the world to me. Yes, of course, I'm writing for fame and fortune—and the all-important beach house—but at the end of the day, it's all about you. Keep in touch at www.deeernst.com.

About the Author

Dee Ernst loved reading at an early age and decided to become a writer, although she admits it took a bit longer than she expected. After the birth of her second daughter at the age of forty, she committed to giving writing a real shot. She loved chick lit but felt frustrated by the younger heroines who couldn't figure out how to get what they wanted, so she writes about women like herself—older, more confident, and with a wealth of life experience. In 2012, her novel *Better Off Without Him* became an Amazon bestseller. Now a full-time writer, Dee lives in her home state of New Jersey with her family, a few cats, and a needy cocker spaniel. She loves sunsets, beach walks, and really cold martinis.